PINEBOX COLLINS

PINEBOX COLLINS

ROD MILLER

THORNDIKE PRESS
A part of Gale, a Cengage Company

Copyright © 2020 by Rod MIller.
All scripture quotations, unless otherwise noted, are taken from the King James Bible.
Thorndike Press, a part of Gale, a Cengage Company.

Thorndike Press® Large Print Western.
The text of this Large Print edition is unabridged.
Other aspects of the book may vary from the original edition.
Set in 16 pt. Plantin.

LIBRARY OF CONGRESS CIP DATA ON FILE.
CATALOGUING IN PUBLICATION FOR THIS BOOK
IS AVAILABLE FROM THE LIBRARY OF CONGRESS

ISBN-13: 978-1-4328-6119-3 (hardcover alk. paper)

Published in 2021 by arrangement with Rod Miller

Printed in Mexico
Print Number: 01   Print Year: 2021

PINEBOX COLLINS

CHAPTER ONE

There's one thing to know about me: a man in my line of work grows accustomed to drinking alone.

And so I have gained the habit over the years of spending my evenings at otherwise empty tables in the far corners of saloons where I can view the festivities from the partial concealment of dim lamplight.

Not that I drink a lot, mind you. I stick to beer and generally nurse a single schooner of an evening until the last sip is flat and tepid. For I have seen what excessive drink can do to a man, and have no desire to suffer the fate they so often do.

At the same time, I never lose sight of the fact that it is whiskey and its abuse that, more often than not, brings business to my door.

The "door" of which I speak is, at present, a rented building on the bluff above, but within sniffing distance of, the river. I reside not far from there, in a rented room sufficient for my needs. In my line of work, being near my place of business at all hours is a convenience if not a requirement, as those needing my services do so no matter the position of the hands on the clock.

While I have, in a sense, the run of the house in which I live, my abode is a single room with sufficient space to accommodate a narrow bed, washstand, wardrobe, an upholstered reading chair, and my steamer trunk. Hanging on the walls are shelves for my books, a shaving mirror, and a peg from which dangles my spare leg and harness.

It occurs that the last of that explanation requires elucidation. And so, we must leave our present environs, if only in our minds, and travel back to the time of my service in the War of the Rebellion. I will make the journey brief and to the point.

I came of age for military service during the unpleasantness and left my home state of Kentucky in 1862 at the age of seventeen to join an Ohio regiment. While a Southern state in its ways and in the sympathies of most residents, you will recall that Kentucky did not secede from the Union and attempted to stay neutral. The attempt proved unsuccessful, with the invasion of a Confederate army followed in short order by an answering invasion from the North. Given the divided loyalties there, it was truly a case of "brother against brother" in Kentucky and so I chose to avoid the confusion and join the fight in support of the Union else-where.

I left the family farm outside of Claryville and journeyed the sixteen miles to Cincinnati, across the river, and then signed on with the 106th Ohio Volunteer Infantry. Damned if they didn't send me right back to Kentucky to fend off an expected attack by Kirby Smith's soldiers that never came. That was in September. By late November, we were garrisoned at Hartsville, Tennessee. I did not see much of the battle, but John Hunt Morgan launched a surprise attack the morning of December 7. For all I know, I may well have been the first casualty, as a cannonball took my right foot as soon as I stood up from my blankets and realized we were in a fight.

Later, I was told the rebs not only had us by surprise, they had us outnumbered. And so, by the time reinforcements arrived from Castalian Springs, they found only a bloody field littered with the dead and wounded of both sides. Morgan and the Confederates were long gone, taking with them wagons full of supplies and ammunition for the ragtag rebel soldiers, and some eighteen hundred prisoners.

Not only had the secessionists taken my right foot, the shoe from my left foot was stolen along with all my clothes save my underwear and what was left of my breeches. They said I was damn lucky I didn't freeze to death, although the cold may have contributed to the clotting of my blood, thus saving me from bleeding out.

A field surgeon performed an amputation — what was then the preferred treatment for most any wound to any extremity — and sawed off my leg below the knee before shipping me off to an army hospital in Nashville. I have no recollection of any of this, save a hazy memory here and there. The hospital surgeons cut the stiff, bloody, crusty bandages from my leg, cleaned out the maggots, and tidied up the battlefield butcher's work as much as possible.

After what they considered a suitable period of convalescence, the army booted me out of the hospital, handed me a $75 allowance toward purchase of an "artificial limb" and mustered me out of the service. Thus ended my military career.

Upon studying the newfangled artificial limbs on offer from manufacturers doing a land-office business in Nashville, surrounded as they were by some dozen military hospitals warehousing nearly seven thousand wounded Union soldiers, I opted to pocket the stipend and fashion my own appendage from a saw log. After all, wooden legs had been propping up people suffering my malady as far back as history records.

And so, with drawknife and chisels and gouges, I joined the parade of peg legs. My early creations were, admittedly, crude. But over the years I have adapted and improved my manufacture and learned to fashion a functional and somewhat comfortable prosthesis. Once I had mastered the mechanics, I turned to the aesthetics and have for years decorated my replacement peg legs with fancy and intricate carvings and designs. A vanity, I confess, but one that brings me pleasure and often inspires comment.

But that is neither here nor there.

Return with me, then, to Nashville, where I found myself one of hundreds, perhaps thousands, of medically discharged soldiers with missing limbs and without prospects. We were the lucky ones. We survived. The dead were always among us, whether expired from battlefield wounds or from taking sick in the camps and hospitals. Ague, the flux, smallpox, bilious fever, lung fever, and a host of other ailments took more

Union and Confederate lives in that war than did the fighting.

Disposing of the dead was, as you might imagine, a chore without end. On the battlefield, it often amounted to nothing more than bodies left behind by the losing side being dumped into shallow, mass graves by the victors; their own dead given little more ceremony other than an individual and often unmarked resting place. The farther from the battlefield a body found itself, the more attention its burial received.

Every care was taken in Nashville to identify those who breathed their last in the hospitals, with notification of kinfolk when time and circumstance allowed. Graveyards filled to overflowing and new burial grounds opened to accommodate the excess. Wealthy Northerners, for whom money was no issue, were often found making rounds in the city in search of a dead son or husband to accompany home for burial. Other like-minded families who could afford to do so made long-distance arrangements for railroad shipment back home of the coffins carrying their departed soldiers.

For all these and other reasons, as the time between death and deposition grew longer, preserving the bodies grew more important. Medical embalming proved most effective, and embalmers and undertakers trained in the practice found steady and plentiful work under contract with grieving families.

And so I sit here alone with my lukewarm lager in the dim corner of this saloon. For, needing work and seeing opportunity in Nashville, I hired on as apprentice to a merchant of grief and then and there took up The Dismal Trade.

CHAPTER TWO

By the end of 1864, the war was all but over in Tennessee. John Bell Hood's rebel army, already weakened from fighting at Franklin, was practically wiped out by Union general George Thomas in Nashville in December. Hood and what was left of his troops high-tailed it south across the Duck River and were seen no more.

By the end of those fights roundabout Nashville I was well-trained in my chosen line of work; if not in time served, then in undertaker duties learned and embalmings accomplished. Therefore, I decided to quit the place and seek opportunity in the West, as would scores of thousands of other war veterans from both camps. With nothing to hold me in Tennessee and no reason to return to Kentucky, I followed the setting sun in pursuit of a fresh start.

For no discernible reason, springtime found me in the Ozarks and the town of

Springfield, Missouri. I shared the city with many former soldiers: soldiers who had worn both the blue and the gray. Soldiers who still wore the uniform of the Union army were not uncommon on the streets of Springfield at the time — given the presence of district headquarters there, as well as an army hospital and government storehouses.

The spring air was thick with tension when I got to town. Saloon squabbles between Northerners and Southerners — or those with such sympathies — were frequent and sometimes resulted in violence. When news of President Lincoln's assassination arrived, cheers and celebrations by Confederates were met with threats by radical Unionists to wipe out the Southern sympathizers. Cooler heads, however, prevailed.

Of note from a strictly personal perspective, the preservation of the late president's body by embalming displayed the technique's efficacy to thousands upon thousands of citizens who viewed his remains in a dozen cities over the three weeks between his death in the nation's capital and interment in the capital of his adopted state of Illinois (Lincoln being, like me, a native of Kentucky). Acceptance of the embalmer's art grew substantially in the aftermath of the assassination.

As spring gave way to summer, rowdiness prevailed in Springfield. Among the most raucous of the unruly was one James Butler Hickok. Many an evening I would leave the solitude of my abode and my books to visit the taverns of the town and seldom would an evening pass without hearing from or about the man deserving of his appellation, "Wild Bill."

Hickok was given to outrageous outbursts on occasion. Drinking and loud argument seemed to be the man's hobbies, frightening women and children on the streets a favorite pastime, and going horseback on sidewalks and even into buildings an occasional diversion.

The stories told about his colorful past were many and, to my way of thinking, not altogether reliable. It was said he originated in Illinois but left there before he'd got all his growth, following a fist fight in which he believed he had killed his foe. He claimed to have ridden with the Jayhawkers in Bleeding Kansas, survived attack by a bear by killing it with his knife, and was a stable hand for the Pony Express and a freighting company. He purported that during a shoot-out at a stage station over a dispute about

16

unpaid bills, he shot and killed two men and wounded another who later died.

As with most men of the day, Wild Bill was said to have done his duty with the military. He served as either a teamster, a scout, a spy, or all that and more. He was first reported in and around Springfield in service to the provost marshal as a detective of some sort. But according to some residents, he spent most of his time in that job reporting soldiers seen drinking on duty or lingering in the town.

By the time I arrived in Springfield his military days were behind him and he earned his keep at the gambling tables — and apparently was skilled at handling the cards. Not being inclined to games of chance, I never saw the man at work at those tables but did overhear many a conversation attesting to his skill, and more than a few complaints questioning his honesty.

While I did not know it at the time, it was a gambling dispute that occasioned my first encounter with Wild Bill Hickok.

Early one evening — or late in the afternoon, if you'd rather — I tired of the work of assembling coffins in my shop and thought to take a stroll into the livelier part of town. I leaned my weary self against one of the arched doorways into the courthouse to watch the comings and goings in the square.

Not far from where I took my rest, a man I did not know stopped and pulled a watch from his pocket, flipped open the lid, and made some show of checking the time. From across the square came a shout: "Davis Tutt, you had best not cross the square packing my watch!" or something to that effect; the exact words escape me.

The man, who I assumed must be Davis Tutt, pocketed the timepiece and I followed his gaze across the square to the source of the shout. I recognized, as would most anyone residing in Springfield at the time, Wild Bill Hickok.

The response from Tutt came not in words. Rather, he pulled his pistol and took aim at Wild Bill, who returned the favor. Smoke roared from the barrels of both revolvers but the shots sounded as one. Wild Bill, unhit, spun in his tracks, leveling his aim at a group of men behind him and saying something to them which I could not hear. My assumption was that they were friends of this man Tutt.

Tutt, in the instant, also turned, and stumbled toward me with blood pouring from a wounded chest, staggering into and collapsing under a neighboring archway. I hobbled over to where he lay, joining a circle of other onlookers. It looked to me that if Davis Tutt wasn't dead already he soon would be. With each fading beat of his heart, blood pulsed from his wounds, further spreading the scarlet stain on his shirtfront. And then the rhythm stopped and the blood only slowly seeped.

"He's dead," some bystander said as he knelt beside Tutt and felt his throat for signs of a heartbeat, "but I reckon we ought to get a doctor here anyhow." I waited and watched onlookers pause and pass until Doc Ebert arrived and verified what any one of the curiosity seekers already knew: Davis Tutt was no longer of this world.

Someone from the marshal's office — I cannot recollect who — walked across the square from where he had been questioning Wild Bill. He leaned over the body, hands propping himself up on his knees, and studied Tutt's bloody and now naked chest, as Doc Ebert had since pulled aside the man's vest and sliced open the shirt and top of his underwear.

After a moment, the lawman said, "He been shot twice?"

"No," Doc said. "The bullet, see, it hit him here on his right side, about where his sixth rib would be, I guess." His finger

19

traced the bullet's path in the air between the wounds. "Came out about the same place over here on the left. My guess is, the man was standing more or less sidewise to where the shot came from. Couldn't say without opening him up, but the bullet likely tore up the blood vessels near his heart. Maybe even nicked the bottom of his heart. He died quick, these folks say," he said with a wave at the circle of people around the body, "so it tore something up pretty bad in there."

The lawman stood and I sidled over to him and explained in a whisper that I was an undertaker and offered my services in removing the body from the unfortunate and very public place where it had fallen in the town square of Springfield. He sucked at his lips and scratched his head for a moment and finally allowed as how that would be all right with him, and that Tutt's remains would be in my charge until and unless whatever kin he had might decide otherwise.

And so, there being no objections, I undertook the task of preparing the body of Davis Tutt for burial. The embalming, I might add, was made difficult by the severity and location of his wounds. A routine procedure, you see, involves displacing blood by injecting embalming chemicals into the right carotid artery in the neck, with the drainage through the neighboring right jugular vein. In Tutt's case, the damaged vessels in his chest did not allow proper passage and distribution of the fluid, requiring what we in the trade call a "multiple-point injection," necessitating, here, use of the femoral artery and vein.

But all that is of no interest, I suppose.

Tutt was laid to rest in Maple Park cemetery.

About the aforementioned gambling dispute leading up to my closest — although somewhat distant — encounter with Wild Bill. As you might imagine, talk about the gunfight was widespread and I listened in to a number of explanations of the incident.

It seems Davis Tutt was a Southerner and veteran of the rebel army. That alone might have been a source of contention between the two. However, it was said that Tutt and Hickok had been, if not friends, at least friendly acquaintances, and shared many a gambling table. Some claimed Wild Bill's familiarity with a younger sister of Tutt was another source of friction. But most laid it off to gambling. Whatever the reason, the two men were at odds.

During a game at the Lion House, at which Tutt was only a bystander offering

21

advice to a friend in hopes he could beat Hickok, Wild Bill prevailed and quit the game with more money than he brought to the table, infuriating Tutt. Tutt demanded Wild Bill use his newfound wealth to repay a $35 debt he owed. Hickok declined, claiming he owed Dave only $25 and said he had a note to prove it.

During the discussion, Tutt grabbed Wild Bill's pocket watch from the table, saying he would hold it as collateral until the debt was satisfied. The watch, for some reason, was an important keepsake of Wild Bill's. He left the card room without it, but with a warning for Tutt: "If you display that watch in public, Dave, I will kill you."

Which he did.

Two days after the shooting, Wild Bill Hickok was arrested for murder. The charge was reduced to manslaughter and for three days he was on trial before a jury, which acquitted him, deeming it a fair fight.

A magazine writer from the East came to town a month or so later and turned Wild Bill into a legend, his story based mostly on lies.

Hickok's days in Springfield were numbered. He ran for marshal, lost the election, and left town to further embellish his newfound fame.

And thus ended my first encounter with the works and ways of Wild Bill Hickok. It would not be the last. And, as we shall see, Wild Bill's last encounter on this earth would be with me.

CHAPTER THREE

Clouds of dust, swarms of flies, the whoops and hollers of cowhands, and the bellering of cattle convinced me to leave Springfield. My time there was as finished as Davis Tutt.

Well, maybe not quite so — I stayed in the city until the following summer. But business was not as brisk as one might hope. Not that people in Springfield weren't dying. They were, as they will. Keep in mind that at the time I was still a young man. A very young man. My face was clean-shaven more by circumstance than choice, as any whiskers that sprouted were as thin and scraggly as a weed patch on hardpan. And it is a fact that folks seeking the services of an undertaker tend to prefer a man whose years lend more solemn dignity than I could muster at my tender age — as if clothing a corpse in a wooden overcoat required a head of hair infused with strands of gray.

I nailed up coffins and embalmed and laid

out such customers as came my way in Springfield as I cast about for opportunities in less-settled environs, where circumstances may mitigate the lack of appeal engendered by my lack of years.

Thus, the aforementioned cattle. Texas cattle, to be precise.

During the summer of 1866, herds of hatchet-headed, slab-sided, dewclaw-rattling longhorn cattle hoofed it through our neighborhood, prodded along their way by grimy young cowboys, trail-worn from some two months in saddle. The cattle were out of Texas, headed for railroad shipment east out of Sedalia, some one hundred miles north of Springfield. Now, driving cattle to market was no new thing. But after the war, northern beef was in short supply, and Texas was overstocked with cattle and undersupplied with money. And so the Texans opened the floodgates with tons of beef on the hoof to balance the scales.

In visiting with the drovers, I was given to understand the dangers of the enterprise. Not so much the things one might expect, such as river crossings and lightning storms and stampeding cattle and the like. But man-made dangers, such as angry Kansas and Missouri farmers stopping herds short at the point of a gun in an attempt to keep what they called Texas fever from infecting their own pen-raised cattle.

Such danger was so intense I was called upon in my professional capacity to prepare for burial a young cowboy who ran afoul of a mob of Missouri "clodhoppers" — as the cowboys sometimes called them — and got shot for his troubles. It seems the young man left the herd one morning in search of a few wandering steers and found, instead, the angry farmers who shot him then tied his body across his saddle with a note pinned to the back of his shirt advising the Texans to quit the country with their infected animals. The horse wandered back to the herd, by then bedded down not far from Springfield, on an evening I happened to be at the cowboy camp for a visit.

I suspect the dead cowboy, a man of about my age who answered to the name of J.D. Boggs, was one of the few Texas drovers to leave this world with a proper burial, if only in a six-board coffin. My only regret was offering my services at a reduced rate. But the ragtag nature of the cowboy company belied the riches that would soon result from the sale of their cattle upon arrival in Sedalia. Had I but known.

A few, but not many, of the cowboys I met that summer in their camps were veterans of the late war, having fought on the side of the Confederacy. Most were too young to have served. Their curiosity about the fighting led to many a fireside conversation, as I shared my limited experience in the actual conflict. And there was a certain morbid fascination about the line of work that resulted from my time in the military.

My peg leg, too, was an item of interest. But what impressed the cowboys more was my means of getting about on horseback. It was simple, really. I had replaced the right stirrup on an otherwise standard-issue McClellan army saddle with a shallow, flat-bottomed, thick leather pouch of my own design, stitched together by a Nashville harness maker. After mounting the horse in the accustomed manner from the left side, I would swing into the seat and slide my wooden appendage into the sleeve as slick as a foot into a stirrup. The fit was snug enough to avoid slippage but not so snug as to hold my wooden leg fast should I, for whatever reason, become unhorsed. Its use allowed my right leg to bear weight for proper balance and control while riding as well as providing a more comfortable seat.

My "stirrup" was by no means a major innovation — I suspect many a man missing all or part of a leg from that war or as far back as men went horseback in stirrups, devised a similar accommodation. Still and all, more than a few of those Texas cowboys found it a fascination, albeit a minor one.

What fascinated me in these encounters came not from the cowboys but from the trail bosses in charge of the herds. The cowboys themselves mostly lacked interest in the bigger picture and seemed content to confine their view to the rear end of a steer. The bosses, however, stood to make a good deal of money for themselves. Therefore, with money at stake, the trail bosses were ever aware of the hazards and rewards of getting cattle to market. The increasing difficulty of dodging sodbusters was making Sedalia — and other markets in Kansas City, Westport, St. Louis, and elsewhere — too risky. The danger of having herds run off and scattered, and the increasing violence against cowboys, demanded change.

Rumor had it that change was coming in the form of one Joe McCoy, who spread the word among the drovers and in communications to Texas that shipping facilities were in the works farther west, in Abilene, Kansas. Rather than the Sedalia Trail, herds would follow the Chisholm Trail, a path created by Cherokee trader Jesse Chisholm through Indian Territory. With Abilene being away from the more settled regions of Kansas, McCoy and his sponsors believed a bet to attract herds to their shipping point would pay off.

And so, as I mentioned earlier, I considered my prospects in Springfield, and the prospects to the west, in Abilene, and concluded to place my bet alongside McCoy's.

Come the spring, I loaded my woodworking tools in a canvas bag, packed my embalming equipment in its case, and secured my clothing and books and scant household goods in a steamer trunk. I arranged passage via stagecoach, train, and stagecoach again to Abilene in the State of Kansas.

The spur line of the Kansas Pacific Railroad to Abilene had yet to reach the town. I stepped off the mud wagon into the dust of the street, looked around, and wondered if the ground on which I stood was, indeed, the purported destination of the coming season's Texas cattle herds. There weren't but maybe a dozen structures, best described as huts, or hovels. Logs — from trees that grew who knows where, but certainly not here — appeared to be the preferred building material. An absence of shingles was apparent, with but one building in sight covered with such. A bird on the wing would find it difficult to locate Abilene, as the earthen roofs on the remaining hovels blended perfectly with the surrounding land. One of the buildings housed something of a store, another an eating house, and a third log structure — the largest in the business district — a saloon. The rest of the buildings, scattered nearby seemingly at random, were homes — using the term loosely.

But along with dust, there was change in the air. A short distance from what passed for Abilene, a tent city housed workers putting up cow pens of lumber so fresh it still seeped sap. Sawn lumber also created the framework for a large two-story hotel McCoy would call "Drover's Cottage" to house the Texas trail bosses and such cowboys as would choose a feather bed over another night in a fetid bedroll.

The foreman overseeing the works for McCoy assured me the boom was just over the horizon, awaiting only the arrival of the rails. Once building materials could ship all the way to Abilene by train, rather than requiring freight wagons for the final leg, commercial enterprises of all kinds would line the thoroughfare newly christened "Texas Street."

The man opined that McCoy would be

willing to erect a small frame building to house an undertaker. "Every town worthy of the name needs someone to plant a bone orchard," he said.

And so, I stowed my worldly goods and set up housekeeping in an abandoned log hut in the town to await the true birth of Abilene. In the interim, I unpacked my woodworking tools and hired on to do finish work at Drover's Cottage. Later, when the predicted construction boom was realized, I did the same for the future Alamo Saloon, which the owners intended to make into a proverbial palace on the prairie. And that it did become — although a bit gaudy in its fixtures for my taste.

The railroad came. Gunshots filled the air, as did the popping of corks from champagne bottles. Cheers, huzzahs, and hurrahs accompanied much backslapping and handshaking. Joe McCoy's grin was brighter than the noonday sun and Abilene's residents — already many more in number than when I arrived, but few in number compared to what the town would soon host — fairly gleamed with anticipation and excitement at the coming of the rails.

Then the cattle came. In 1867, some thirty-five thousand of the gangly longhorns left Abilene aboard trains hauling them to slaughter. The following year the number of beeves more than doubled, and so did the number of rowdy cowboys leading — or following — them up the trail from Texas. Even more showed up in 1869. Whores and gamblers, crooks and con men came to meet them. Abilene was a wild, wide-open town and fights with fists and knives and guns were ever-present, and blood flowed like whiskey so long as the cowboys were in town.

A headstone city — the "stones" made primarily of carved wood — grew almost as quickly as the town. It does not speak well of me to say so, but every grave filled, every coffin covered, every body embalmed meant money in my pocket. Even with the expense of shipping embalming chemicals, lumber for coffins, fabrics for lining them, and paints and varnishes for finishing the eternity boxes, I prospered.

But, as was typical of the permanent residents of Abilene, I also detested the drovers and the violence they brought with them. Any and all attempts to control the celebrating cowboys in the lawless town fell short. Abilene finally incorporated as a city in September of 1869 and, to no one's surprise, Joe McCoy won the vote to be mayor of his city. Among his first building projects was a jail — a strong, tight lockup with stone walls. But before the walls reached their top, cowboys on a spree knocked them down to a pile of rubble.

Lawlessness did abate somewhat the following summer when McCoy hired Tom "Bear River" Smith out of Colorado to head up law enforcement. Smith was a tough customer. He posted regulations prohibiting firearms, and enforced them mostly with his fists.

Less than half a year later, however, the rowdies had had enough of law and order. In the course of arresting a murderer, Smith took a bullet and returned the favor, wounding his assailant. But the murderer's sidekick whacked the lawman over the head, knocking him senseless to the ground, then picked up an ax and missed chopping off Bear River Smith's head by a shred of skin and the odd tendon or two.

Readying the man's body for burial in such a condition presented difficulties this undertaker had never before undertaken.

Winter was fairly peaceful and quiet in Abilene with the cowboys gone south. While the drovers made ready to launch next season's invasion, the city prepared its defenses, and in the spring of 1871 hired a new man to enforce the law.

His name: James Butler "Wild Bill" Hickok.

CHAPTER FOUR

"Stepping out" with a young lady is not so easy for a mutilated man stumping about on a peg leg. Going for a walk is difficult. Dancing, impossible. Even a carriage ride can prove awkward. It is a rare member of the fairer sex who will accept any overtures from a cripple.

Such a rare member was Maggie. Maggie's father, Brendan O'Malley, pounded steel and bent horseshoes in Abilene as the town's blacksmith. But Maggie's emerald eyes, ginger hair, and freckled face fairly shone above the counter at Goldstein's General Mercantile.

I visited the store nearly every day just for an opportunity to exchange a word with the girl. At age seventeen, Maggie glowed with blooming womanhood. Perhaps not a beauty in the accepted sense, her allure was much stronger, enhanced by the sparkle in her eye, the wrinkle in her nose when she smiled, and the way she had of bowing her head and fixing upon you a gaze filtered through thick lashes, then blinking leisurely as she averted her eyes.

I first saw Maggie at Goldstein's in the winter; then in the spring and into the summer, we spent many a pleasant evening atop my one-horse shay gallivanting about the prairie. Sunday afternoons often found us using the shade of the shay as cover for a picnic lunch.

As shy as she was inviting, her reticence made Maggie, to me, a blank book. And so, in my infatuation, I filled those pages with feelings that mirrored my own. She listened intently to my dreams, my aspirations, nodding from time to time — a reaction I read as understanding, even agreement.

Most telling, she never, not once, expressed revulsion at my line of work as so many are wont to do. That, too, I recorded as acceptance in my so-called "Book of Maggie."

Not that my work interfered with my distraction. While Abilene had grown like a litter of pigs, the increasing population consisted largely of people of an age to have escaped death by childhood disease and not yet ready to succumb to the infirmities of advanced age. And with the cowboys safely in Texas, the death rate from violence in town required no overtime on my part. As well, some, in Abilene as elsewhere, were not yet ready to accept the advantages of embalming, or even the services of an undertaker. The time-tested — and, to my way of thinking, timeworn — technique of laying out a body on a cooling board in the home until danger of premature interment passed still saw use in the community. Oh, the sale of caskets to such families still contributed to my livelihood, and the money on deposit at the Bank of Abilene I accumulated in more prosperous seasons proved more than sufficient to keep the wolf from my door.

Not even the arrival of the gunslinger Wild Bill Hickok and his appointment as marshal in April had contributed to the burial business as yet. But I suspected it soon would, given my brief experience with the man, bolstered by the reputation he had gained in the ensuing years.

Upon leaving Springfield those years ago, Hickok had been, if overheard stories in Abilene's saloons were to be believed, a busy man. As you will recall, he left Missouri after an unsuccessful attempt at election as sheriff of Green County. They say Wild Bill hired on with the army as a scout for General George Armstrong Custer's Seventh Cavalry, during which time he killed several Indians and suffered a wound in the foot when stabbed by a warrior's lance. Unlike me, however, Hickok retained his appendage, which, if my observations were accurate, had healed nicely with no loss of its use.

An incident set in Nebraska defies credibility to the point one is inclined to write it off to the puffery and purple prose of the authors of dime novels featuring a heroic Hickok, but many swore it a true story. While in a Nebraska saloon, Wild Bill argued with a group of four cowboys over a spilled drink. Inviting them to step outside to face off in the street, he outdrew and outshot the men, killing three with bullets to the head and disabling the fourth with bullets that shattered his jaw and shoulder.

The gunfighter's reputation next earned him appointment as a deputy United States marshal in Hays, Kansas, where he later won election as city marshal then won, and again lost, the office of sheriff of Ellis County. If the stories are to be believed, he whittled three more notches on his pistol grip in shooting scrapes there.

A misbehaving man in his cups shooting up Hays was advised by onlookers to cease and desist, or Hickok would lock him up. The man only laughed, mounted his horse, and with rifle in hand, set out to find and kill the lawman. Upon finding him, he brought his rifle barrel to bear.

"Don't shoot him!" Wild Bill hollered to an imaginary someone behind the would-be assailant. "He's only drunk and I will arrest him!"

The drunkard reined his horse around to confront the threat Wild Bill was warning off, giving Hickok time and opportunity to put a bullet in his head.

He shot and killed another inebriated cowboy causing a ruction in a saloon, and in a fracas with a quartet of soldiers — who were having the best of him, it was said — killed one and wounded the other three.

Thus, when Wild Bill Hickok rode into Abilene and pinned on "Bear River" Smith's old badge with a charge to control the town when the cattle herds came, I anticipated an uptick in business.

I would not be disappointed.

It is no surprise, I suppose, that Maggie was enamored with Wild Bill. He was tall, a flashy dresser, and walked with a confident swagger. Then there were those perfumed curls hanging below his shoulders. Something about the man attracted women —

and many men, for that matter — as if they were falling apples and he was the Earth.

At first it was business as usual with Hickok as marshal. He enforced the gun law, settled minor disputes, and patrolled the town. He made his influence felt along Texas Street — and in the many saloons, gambling parlors, and other businesses that lined its boardwalks and spilled over onto adjoining streets. But when the cattle started coming — there would be some seven hundred thousand head shipped that season — he retreated to the Alamo Saloon, which, for all practical purposes, became his office, where he congregated with a rough crowd of gamblers, alcoholists, and frilly representatives of Abilene's demimonde.

Oh, he performed his duties in a way, I suppose. Cowboys understood that there would be no gunplay, and that drunken antics that became destructive would not be tolerated. Beyond that, he made no attempt to root out the corruption that made Texas Street and its environs so distasteful to the ordinary citizens of the town. At the same time, they admired, even idolized, the peacock entrusted with keeping the peace.

It should have come as no surprise, then, when the normally reticent Maggie started singing Wild Bill's praises. Like so many others, she was not immune to his apparent charms and became entwined in his web. At first, it was the mere passing along of gossip about his activities.

"Did you hear how Wild Bill disarmed that band of drovers at the Bull's Head Saloon?"

"They say Wild Bill stepped into the middle of a fistfight last night at the very risk of his life and broke it up!"

"Wild Bill ran a dishonest gambler out of the Alamo Saloon at the point of his gun!"

"I heard Wild Bill saved a dance hall girl from a beating!"

For the most part, I ignored her admiration of Hickok, much as I did that of others in the town. Had I paid more attention, I might have wondered at her fascination with, and attraction to, events on the wilder side of Abilene. And I should have known, I suppose, that whatever charms a one-legged undertaker possessed would pale in comparison to the vigor and vitality of the man who strutted along Texas Street with his pearl-handled revolvers on display.

But, back to business.

The marshal's disallowing of firearms in the city tamped down gun violence, so I did not see as much demand for my services at my storefront embalming parlor as I had anticipated. But still, business did improve. One tragic incident, in fact, required my disposal of two bodies brought down by bullets — all fired from the barrels of Wild Bill's twin revolvers.

It started when Phil Coe came to town.

CHAPTER FIVE

The last time I saw Phil Coe he was lying on his back, dressed in a suit, hands folded lightly over his breast. I studied him for a moment, smoothed the lapel of his jacket, then closed the lid and screwed it down tight. There would be no grave dug for Coe in Abilene. His earthly remains were due for shipment to Prairie Lea, Texas, where family would lay him to eternal rest. Having thoroughly embalmed the corpse, I was confident it would reach Texas and the grave with minimal decomposition.

Coe showed up in the cow town of Abilene late in the spring. Word was the Texan had been a soldier and various other things, but these days made his living as a gambler. He was also said to be a fearsome gunfighter, and in Abilene he fell in with others of that ilk.

Not long after coming to town, he went partners with gunman Ben Thompson to open the Bull's Head Saloon. A rowdy and rough drinking and gambling house, the Bull's Head was typical of other Texas Street saloons, lacking the so-called finery of the Alamo. Barely a night passed after cattle herds started arriving in town without a fracas of some sort breaking out at the Bull's Head. Thompson and Coe did little to discourage the raucous behavior. So long as they poured enough of what passed for whiskey and took their cut from the women and the gambling money, they seemed content to let the cowboys celebrate.

The Bull's Head was a thorn in Wild Bill's side. The owners posted an oversized advertising sign atop the front of the building displaying a longhorn bull ready to fulfill his duties as a sire in every aspect of his anatomy. As you might imagine, the townspeople found the sign distasteful and demanded its removal. Thompson and Coe refused. The city fathers did not care to push the gunfighters, now numbering three with arrival of the notorious murderer John Wesley Hardin. The job fell to Wild Bill.

Our town marshal led a short parade down Texas Street, two men carrying a ladder trailed by a third with a bucket of paint. I joined a handful of the curious in their wake. Without ceremony, Hickok, a sawed-off shotgun cradled in his elbow, instructed the placement of the ladder. No sooner was it leaned against the building than the door swung open and Thompson, Coe, and Hardin stepped off the boardwalk and onto the street. A half dozen or so cowboys followed, some with drink in hand.

Thompson looked on with half a smile on his face. Coe did not see the humor in the situation.

"What the hell you up to, Hickok?"

Wild Bill looked at Coe, looked up at the sign, watched paintbrush and bucket make its way up the ladder in the hand of a man who seemed in no hurry to reach the top, and looked back at Coe. He smiled. "Why, Phil, I'm just here to see to the improvement of your sign. Mayor and town council told you folks to fix it, but they tell me you were not so inclined. Told them I was not afraid of a little dab of paint. So, here I am."

"You touch that sign and I will shoot you where you stand."

Coe's determination caused the crowd to shift, clearing the street behind the marshal.

Hickok smiled again, breaking the silence only with the snick of the shotgun's hammers as he drew them back with a thumb.

"You don't scare me, Wild Bill. Why not toss that scattergun aside and we'll have it out right here and now with our pistols?"

Again, Wild Bill smiled and turned his attention to the man on the ladder. His brushwork left much to be desired in the way of neatness, and the colors did not match. But more of the bull's offending organ disappeared with every stroke.

"Well?" Coe said.

Wild Bill's smile as he looked at Coe only made the saloonkeeper look all the angrier. "Smile, you sonofabitch! Had you ever seen me shoot, you wouldn't find this here situation so amusing."

"Is that right, Phil?"

"You're damn right that's right. I can shoot a crow right out of the sky and kill him deader'n hell."

Again, Will Bill smiled. "Tell me something, Phil — would that crow be carrying a gun? And would he be shooting back at you? You had best think about that, for if you come after me, I sure as hell will be."

Had Hickok been made of candle wax, he would have melted in the heat of Coe's stare. Thompson and Hardin sidled over to Coe, and Thompson whispered something that took Coe's mad down a notch.

I took a few steps closer to the trio as they watched the painter come down the ladder, watching them over his shoulder as he descended. As the rest of the crowd drifted away, I heard Coe's anger bubble up again and boil over.

"That highfalutin sonofabitch Hickok needs to die," he said. "One of us is going to have to kill him."

Thompson said, "I ain't got no beef with Bill. I leave him alone and he leaves me alone and him and me get along fine."

"If you want him killed you're going to have to do it yourself," Hardin said. "Hell, I kind of like ol' Wild Bill."

"Yeah, I seen you fawning around that uppity bastard."

"We have a drink now and then. Maybe play a hand of cards. Ain't no harm in that."

"You think so? Wild Bill ain't nothin' but a damn Yankee. He don't like Southerners and hates Texans especially. Come to it, he'd as soon shoot you as look at you."

Hardin clapped a hand on Coe's shoulder. "More likely he'll be shooting at you, Phil. And when he does, I suspect he'll kill you."

Coe tossed Hardin's hand off and stomped back into the Bull's Head, casting a nasty look at the formerly nasty advertising sign as he went.

"Wild Bill!" Hardin said. "Buy you a drink?"

"Sure thing. C'mon down to the Alamo."

Phil Coe was correct in his assessment of Hardin's admiration of the marshal. Although a known killer and feared gunman in his own right, John Wesley Hardin seemed envious of Wild Bill's reputation. He questioned Hickok about his gunfights and hung on Wild Bill's every word. According to talk I overhead from the Texas cowboys, Hardin might have the edge over Wild Bill in terms of the number of men killed. But, if the stories are to be believed, Hardin was more murderer than gunfighter.

John Wesley Hardin, son of a Methodist preacher and named for John Wesley, the religionist of long times past who founded the sect, betrayed no hint of a moral upbringing. One afternoon, I heard a drover in the Alamo say he was from Hardin's hometown of Bonham, and that Hardin drew first blood at age fifteen when he shot and killed a freed slave. "Didn't just kill him," the cowboy said. "Shot him five times to make sure he was dead." He went on to relate how John Wesley quit town, pursued by three soldiers sent to arrest him. Hardin ambushed and killed all three.

Other cowboys told tales of their own. In Towash, Hardin killed a man in an argument over a card game. He went to a circus in Horn Hill, argued with and shot and killed another patron after a disagreement. Refused to pay a pimp for the services of a prostitute, then shot him. Killed a lawman in Waco, and when hunted down and arrested for the crime, somehow managed to kill his captor and stole his horse to escape. Shot a Mexican trail boss on a cattle drive when his herd got too close to the one Hardin was with — Hardin's herd being made up of rustled cattle, according to the cowboy who told the story.

If all the stories are to be believed, Hardin was a man to watch out for. But, as I said, he did not challenge Hickok. The marshal warned him about carrying guns, and Hardin complied for the most part. His twin holsters, hitched cross-draw style to the front of his vest in a fashion I had never seen before nor ever seen since, were mostly empty in the streets of Abilene.

But Hardin's guns eventually got him on Wild Bill's bad side.

On a hot August night, John Wesley was on a spree with a cousin and a friend. They drank and gambled their way up and down Texas Street, finally staggering off to the American House Hotel to sleep it off. Hardin and his cousin shared a room and their friend bunked up next door.

Unable to sleep owing to the snores rattling through the wall, Hardin yelled and pounded on the wall and hollered repeatedly for quiet. When the racket continued, Hardin pulled a pistol from a drawer and emptied the cylinder through the wall.

The snoring stopped. As did all sound from next door. Hardin, in his underwear, went next door to find that one of his bullets had hit the sleeping man in the head.

When I was sent to fetch the body later, Hardin's cousin told me what happened.

"Scared poor John Wesley so bad he jumped out the window 'thout even stoppin' to get dressed!" he said. "Hid out in that haystack yonder till after Wild Bill went away. Then come by and said through the window he was all for lightin' out for Texas. Done borrowed a horse from the hitch rail at the Bull's Head and left town on a high lope."

And so ended John Wesley Hardin's sojourn in Abilene.

His dead friend, on the other hand, never did leave town. With Hardin's bullet still in his head, I buried him in a six-board coffin in a grave with a wooden marker.

After Hardin left town, Hickok and Phil Coe continued their waltz toward a confrontation. Over the summer, Hickok held court at the Alamo, Coe at the Bull's Head. I don't know why he did it. He had sold his interest to Thompson but stayed on running the tables. While Texas cowboys caroused in all the drinking establishments, they always found the warmest welcome at the Bull's Head. While I visited there from time to time, my wooden appendage too often drew ridicule from the rowdy element that frequented the Bull's Head.

Under the circumstances, and despite my ambivalence toward Wild Bill Hickok, I found the more refined atmosphere at the Alamo more congenial on those evenings when my books refused to hold my interest. Those very words, "more refined atmosphere," are an absurd description of the saloon, which was unruly enough, but in comparison to the Bull's Head, it is apt. With empty tables as rare as hair on a billiard ball, a chair in the corner of the Alamo kept me somewhat away from the fray and offered a ringside seat as well as a listening station.

One October evening, as the last of the cattle herds of the season were arriving in Abilene, Texas Street seemed extra boisterous. Propped in the corner of the Alamo nursing a stale mug of beer in which the foam had long since dissipated, I sat watching saloon girls sashay around advertising their wares, overhearing cowboy yarns, hearing the clickety-clack of the roulette wheel and the whir of shuffling cards, and listening to the groans of gamblers who lost and the whoops of the winners. I heard the sound of gunfire in the street and saw Wild Bill perk up at the noise. He took to his feet in a trice and headed for the door ahead of a crowd of which I became a part, stumping along on my peg leg in an effort to keep up.

"Phil, what the hell's going on here?" Wild Bill hollered, hands perched upon the butts of his holstered revolvers.

Phil Coe stood in the street, trying to stay steady but having little luck. He swayed back and forth, a still-smoking pistol in hand. A scattering of four or five cowhands wobbled nearby.

"I plead self-defense, Marshal," Coe said. "I was under attack by a mangy cur and shot at it to protect myself."

"A dog, you say?"

"A dog it is, Wild Bill." Coe waved his gun around toward his cowboy contingent. "These Texas gentlemen stand as my witnesses."

The cowboys concurred with Coe, offering various claims and opinions as to the imminent threat offered by the perilous mongrel.

"Well, Phil, it looks as if the dog is gone. I will have your pistol now."

"Like hell you will," Coe said as the swaying barrel made its way toward the lawman. The cowboys lent their voices to Coe's refusal to disarm.

Wild Bill said, "Come on now, Phil. You know firearms ain't allowed in the street."

Coe laughed. "Do declare! What, then, are them things strapped around you, there?" The unsteady barrel of his pistol served as a pointer.

Hickok took a step toward Coe.

Coe let loose a shot.

Wild Bill pulled a pistol and fired twice at Coe. He did not miss.

Aware of the angry cowboys, Hickok kept his gun drawn, his eyes darting here and there in search of a threat. At the sound of running footsteps on the boardwalk behind him, he wheeled and shot.

Mike Williams, one of Wild Bill's deputies, fell dead.

Hickok paled, holstered his gun, and knelt beside the man who was only answering the call of a law officer — to run toward the sound of gunfire, while all others take the opposite route.

"Sonofabitch," the marshal said in less

than a whisper.

I hobbled my way to the office and fetched my cart. Bystanders still milled around in shock, a few townspeople having joined the now-quiet cowboys. They helped lift the body of Mike Williams into what they rudely called my "meat wagon." But no one called it that on this night. No one, in fact, had anything to say.

I expected Phil Coe would join Williams at my establishment. But there were still signs of life in the gunfighter who had gambled and lost, and some of his cowboy friends hustled him off to the doctor's office.

He lasted three days. Mike Williams was already in the ground when Coe took his place on my table.

The death of the deputy spelled the end of Wild Bill Hickok in Abilene. The town council asked for, and got, his badge. Fed up with the annual violence, finding it too steep a price to pay for the wealth the cattle herds brought with them, the townsfolk, residents of the town Joe McCoy built for cattle, let it be known through their elected officers that trail herds were no longer welcome in Abilene.

Unbeknownst to me, unexpected, even, the deaths of Mike Williams and Phil Coe also meant the demise of Maggie and me.

When Coe finally succumbed and I had him laid out for embalming, Maggie knocked at my door. I set aside the pump, stripped off my gloves, and hung my apron.

"Maggie! What is it?"

She met my wide eyes only briefly, then dipped her head and looked at me through her eyelashes in that way she had.

"I want to see him."

"Who?"

"Phil Coe."

It took a moment.

"What did you say? I don't think I heard you right."

"I want to see Phil Coe's body."

Still, I could not make sense of it. "Maggie. Whatever for?"

Now the loss for words seemed to be hers.

"It's Wild Bill," she said after a moment, then pressed her lips into a thin line.

"Wild Bill? Whatever do you mean?"

"He's leaving, you know."

"Yes, I know. So?"

Maggie cleared her throat, more to collect her thoughts, I think, than for any other reason. "I guess you know I admire him."

"I have thought so. Although I cannot imagine why."

"He is a brave man. I find that — I don't

know — stimulating, I suppose."

Again, I searched for a response. "But what has that to do with Phil Coe?"

"It is hard to say. Wild Bill killed him. I suppose I am curious. I want to see the result of his work."

I could only shake my head.

"Why not?"

"Well, for one thing, it's indecent. He is at this moment, unclothed. Not a sight fit for a young lady."

"He's dead. He won't care. Why should you?"

"It's not decent. His body is as naked as the day he was born."

"Do the bullet holes show?"

"Of course they do."

"Both of them?"

I nodded.

"I want to see them. I want to see what Wild Bill did."

Again, I could only stare. After a moment, "I'm sorry, Maggie. You have interrupted my work. I must get back to it."

I closed the door. It proved to be as final as the closing of the lid on Phil Coe's coffin.

CHAPTER SIX

Many a night I awake from fitful sleep with a painful itch in my right foot. Sometimes, half-awake, I reach down to scratch and relieve the irritation only then to realize — remember — the foot is not there. Strange as it may sound, in some odd way the foot *is* still there. My body imagines it to be where it belongs. Even more strange, its presence is required if I am to walk on my peg leg.

On those mornings when I do not feel my absent foot and the part of the leg to which it was attached, I pinch myself on the right thigh, perhaps give it a few smart slaps. Then, for reasons I do not understand, the rest of me believes the missing parts are back where they belong, and walking on wood is possible. It is, I suppose, some recompense for the pain that comes in the night. Upon arriving in Kansas City, I found my nights, as often as not, more restless than restful, owing to the phantom pain — and for other reasons.

Shortly after seeing to the shipping of Phil Coe out of Abilene in his coffin, I tore down my shingle and used the broken boards to warm my sleeping room during my last night in the cow town. Come the morning, I cleaned and packed my embalming equipment into its case, my woodworking tools in their bag, my books and clothing and household goods into the steamer trunk, and boarded the eastbound Kansas Pacific Railway train.

I disembarked in Kansas City, seeking the anonymity not available in Abilene. The city, once nothing more than a typical Missouri-Kansas border burg, had blossomed a few years earlier when chosen as the site of the Hannibal & St. Joseph Railroad Bridge to span the Missouri River. That, and the construction of sprawling stockyards, made the place something of a boomtown, the population swelling to near thirty-five thousand souls by the time I arrived. While leaving Abilene separated me from Texas cowboys, it created no distance between me and Texas cattle. Sometimes, when the wind was right, the stink from the stockyards far surpassed that of Abilene.

My home in Kansas City was a Grand

Avenue boardinghouse. Most days I spent sequestered in my room with my books or bundled up on the back porch. I had accumulated enough money that, while not well off by any means, I had no need — or desire — to seek employment. My embalming equipment remained packed away. I did, however, put my woodworking and carving tools to some use.

A single chunk of fine-grained oak commanded my attention over the course of several weeks. My peg leg, a simple, square, tapered affair bottoming out in a rounded block, showed considerable signs of wear, with splinters and chips missing here and there. And so, needing a replacement, I approached the job with something more unusual in mind. Perhaps owing to whimsy, or maybe as a tip of the hat to the cattle trade, for whatever reason I set out to fashion a stump in the style of the front leg of a steer. Obtaining a model was simple enough, requiring only a trip to the stockyards and — with permission, of course — removing the lower limb from an animal in the dead pile.

I shaped and smoothed the wood to mirror the form of the bovine foreleg from the knee down: the shank, dewclaws, a slight slope to the pastern, and the hoof, carved to appear cloven but in fact solid throughout. I did not paint or stain my new prosthetic leg — only oiled the oak to preserve it and enhance its natural beauty.

If any other such appendage existed on the missing limb of any of the thousands so maimed during the late war, it never came to my attention. I only know the time spent carving the prosthesis kept my mind and hands occupied in such a way that allowed more unpleasant thoughts and memories to fall away like wood shavings as I fashioned the leg.

Such would prove to be the case on other occasions — but I am getting ahead of myself.

The handsome new appendage attracted some notice the rare times I ventured into the streets or took a meal at a café or a quiet drink in a barroom. Curious stares, for the most part. A smile and shake of the head at times. And, rarely, outright laughter. But, being accustomed to gawking, I took it all in stride, so to speak, finding levity less insulting than pity.

After a time, as my finances dwindled and my mind accepted the notion, it became necessary to once again earn my way in the world. I did not care, at the time, to open an undertaking business of my own, nor did practicing the embalmer's art in the employ of an established firm appeal. Rather, I set out to visit the city's undertakers and ply them with offers of supplying coffins. Some refused, believing it more profitable to craft their own, or because the carpentry involved preceded their entrée into undertaking. For some, in fact, laying out the dead was secondary to cabinetry.

But there were undertakers who accepted my offer, and over time I earned a reputation for dependability and fair prices, even to the point of winning over some previously reluctant prospects. My expenses in setting up the enterprise were minimal, as I already owned the necessary tools and, for a slight increase in my room and board at the Grand Avenue rooming house, was given use of a small shed in the side yard.

The cards I printed up to publicize the business listed my name as Jonathon Collins, but given my trade, customers soon started calling me "Pinebox" Collins. At first I tried to dissuade use of the name, pointing out that pine wood only figured into the construction of the cheaper coffins, with walnut, oak, cherry, maple, poplar, and lumber from other trees more typical. But, logic notwithstanding, it proved a fruitless effort. The moniker "Pinebox" Collins stuck, and in time I grew accustomed to it and even adopted it for my own use.

My work in Kansas City seldom put me in direct contact with the public. Most mourners chose "off-the-shelf" coffins, and those with specific wishes communicated them through the undertaker. And so it was with some surprise that I received a note from an errand boy requesting my presence at City Hospital.

With the assistance of a nurse, I found the sender in the men's ward. Sitting up in bed, he appeared healthy enough save a thick bandage wrapped around the stump of his left arm. Although it looked to be several layers deep, the white of the wrapping was stained in spots with seeping blood.

The man introduced himself. "Mister Collins, I am Matthew Brooks. It is unlikely you know me. I run a farm out toward Westport."

"How can I help you, Mister Brooks?"

"Matthew, please."

"Yes, sir. And you can call me 'Pinebox.' Most folks do. What happened to your arm?"

"It's like this. We're putting up hay, you see. There's a newfangled contraption called a hay baler the implement dealer brought out to the place to demonstrate. Made by

62

the same company as makes the McCor-
mick reaper, you see.

"Anyhow, I was pitching hay into the maw
of that clattering contraption when I
slipped. Stuck out my arm to catch myself,
don't you know, and got it tangled up in the
works. Mangled it so bad before they could
shut the machine down that the doc said
there weren't nothing to be done but ampu-
tate. Sawed it off above the elbow, as you
can see."

I nodded, understanding his story but still
unsure why it should matter to me. I guess
the look on my face said as much.

"A friend of mine, he's an undertaker."

Again, I nodded but had nothing to say.

"He tells me you build coffins. Says you're
good at it."

Another nod.

"What I want, Pinebox, is for you to build
me a coffin."

I felt my eyes go wide, and from the look
on Matthew Brooks's face, I could see he
saw it. He laughed.

"No, it ain't for me. And there ain't
nobody else dead, least as far as I know."

He let that sink in for a time before
continuing. I could see he took pleasure in
my confusion.

Then, "This here arm I ain't got no more

63

is on ice somewhere down the basement of this here infirmary. What I want is for you to build a box for it, a coffin," he said, again waggling the stump. "That's what you do, ain't it?"

It took a moment. "Yes, sir, I do build coffins. But I have never been called upon to build one such as you request."

He opined as how building a smaller version of an eternity box should not be beyond my capabilities and I had to agree. I took the measure of his remaining arm. The practical aspects of the job required little discussion, but we spent considerable time talking about his desired flourishes and fancies. I suggested burled maple as an attractive wood for the job, and allowed that I had a fine-looking slab on hand.

I agreed to frame the box with decorative molding carved in the appearance of twisted rope. He requested interior padding and satin lining and polished brass hardware. He went so far as to admire the workmanship of my steer leg, saying it gave him confidence that I should have no trouble meeting his expectations. I could not name a price on the spot, given the unusual nature of the project, but offered to do some figuring and come back later in the day with the cost.

"Not to worry. I'll pay your bill no matter. I trust you'll treat me fair."

We shook hands and I turned to leave, then turned back with a question.

"May I ask, sir, why you want this?"

"I'll answer that with a question of my own. Where did you lose your leg?"

"Tennessee. Hartsville."

"The war, I presume?"

I nodded.

"Ever wonder what happened to it?"

After a moment's consideration, I answered with furrowed brow. "Not really. Cannonball took care of most of it, I should imagine. After most battles, there were piles of arms and legs outside the field surgeons' tents. What was left of mine ended up in one of those heaps, I suppose, to be buried when time allowed."

Matthew Brooks thought about that for a bit. "Well, son," he said. "You're a heap younger than me. I suppose over the years I've grown more attached to my arm. It has served me well and done a heap of work for me, and I guess I just want to see it laid to rest with some measure of respect."

I nodded and turned again to go. This time he interrupted my leaving with a chuckle. "Besides," he said, "my wife thinks I've gone 'round the bend with such a notion, and I cannot resist giving the old girl the satisfaction."

The undersized coffin for interment of Matthew Brooks's arm met with his approval and I was invited to the brief ceremony — which became something of a celebration — as it was laid to rest in a shady grove on his farm. Then it was back to my usual routine of filling orders for coffins of a more typical size. Late most afternoons would find me tipped back in a chair, peg leg propped on the porch rail, book in hand.

But, more and more often, I would go out and wander the streets of Kansas City, watching buildings growing out of the prairie like bluestem grass. I also grew more accustomed to the interiors of a goodly number of its drinking establishments. But, as I had grown accustomed to do in my undertaking days, I was content to hold back — to bide my time observing the goings-on from a quiet corner rather than engage with the other patrons.

Come the end of summer, visitors deluged Kansas City. They came from far and near, by the thousands and tens of thousands to celebrate the Kansas City Industrial Exposition.

Among the visitors was a man I had

known of from my days in Springfield and known from my time in Abilene: James Butler "Wild Bill" Hickok.

CHAPTER SEVEN

I had heard rumors from time to time that Wild Bill was in Kansas City, plying his trade as a gambler. Owing to the size of the city, I thought it unlikely we should cross paths. That, and the fact that the gambling halls professional gamblers frequented were a world removed from the quiet, neighborhood taverns I visited on occasion. The object of the penny-ante poker games there was more a matter of companionship and camaraderie than a means of livelihood.

But one afternoon in late September I made my way to the Twelfth Street entry into the second annual presentation of the Kansas City Industrial Exposition. Tens of thousands of curiosity seekers covered the nearly one hundred acres of the Exposition grounds. And there were plenty of attractions to satisfy — or pique — their curiosity. Horse races, baseball contests, farmers showing off livestock, mothers showing off babies, works of art, farm implements, and all manner of things were on display.

There I was, one among thousands in the crowd, minding my business and studying a complicated new contraption called a sewing machine, when someone tapped on my shoulder and said, "Say there, ain't you that corpse collector from over Abilene way?"

I turned, and lo and behold it was Wild Bill Hickok himself. Rather than holsters, his twin six-shooters were tucked cross-draw style into a shiny red sash around his middle.

"Wild Bill — Mister Hickok —" I managed to sputter.

"Sakes alive, it is you. Sorry I don't recollect your name."

I swallowed hard. "Collins. Jonathon. Folks have taken to calling me 'Pinebox.' "

He clapped me on the shoulder and offered to treat me to a lemonade.

"Me?" I said, as if he could have meant anyone else. "Why me?"

Hickok smiled. "Hell, son, you're the only soul I know in Kansas City who would sit down with me and not want to take my money — or wonder if he could best me in a gunfight."

We shaded up under a commodious canvas roof, found a vacant table, and sat. I asked Wild Bill what he'd been up to.

"Well, son, I been hangin' around Kansas City some, playing cards and whatnot. Now and then I hire on with some greenhorns to guide a hunting trip out on the prairies." He paused to sip his lemonade and used the side of a finger to mop the residue from his mustaches. "Son, you ever been to Niagara Falls?"

"Niagara Falls? No, sir."

"Well you ought to see that place. They dump more water over them falls in a minute than what flows through the whole state of Nevada and most of Utah Territory in a year's time — hell, ever, maybe. Anyways, I was up there at that place a month or so back. Over on the Canada side, we was, huntin' buffalo."

My confusion must have been apparent on my face, as Hickok watched me with a sly smile for a while. "All for show, son. All for show. Some fellow name of Sidney Barnett was behind the whole thing. Got Buffalo Bill Cody in on the deal — Billy and me, we been friends since I took the boy under my wing back when we both worked for Russell, Majors, and Waddell. Texas Jack Omorhundo was in on the show for a time, but quit the deal when getting buffalo to Niagara Falls proved a harder job than anyone thought.

"The whole thing finally got organized, and I was to act as master of ceremonies. Was to be a buffalo hunt, like I said, and some showing off of cowboy work. Whole thing turned out to be a joke. Four buffalo, and them pen-raised," Hickok said with a laugh. "I rode around swinging a *reata* trying to goad an old ox to run so's I could rope it. The Mexican vaqueros and cowboys who was part of the show didn't have any better luck tryin' to chase steers. Buffalo Bill and the Indians couldn't get them four buffalo to run neither. The mighty hunters just milled around shooting their bows. Them in the crowd was in more danger of gettin' hit with a stray arrow than the buffalo was of gettin' shot.

"Anyhow, we put on a couple of shows as advertised and I drew my pay and come on back here. Barnett, he lost a good deal of money on the deal, but he paid me, so that's all I care about. I don't care much for the entertainment business. Buffalo Bill, now, he likes that sort of thing and talked some of puttin' together a big show someday."

Wild Bill again paused to sip his lemonade. "As for now, Cody says he is startin' up a stage show with Texas Jack to tour around the cities back east. Goin' to call it

'Scouts of the Prairie.' Wants me to join up with what he calls his 'Combination' but I ain't so sure. Might give it a try sometime."

Fingering a slice of lemon out of his glass, Hickok folded it in half and bit down on the pulp. Despite all the sugar in the mixture, it must have had some sour left in it, as he wagged his head and blubbered his lips. He cast the peel aside and asked about my doings since leaving Abilene. "As I recollect, you was sweet on that little Irish gal worked at Goldstein's store. Thought by now you'd be harnessed to that woman and fixin' to start up a family — if them Johnny Rebs didn't shoot off more'n your foot, that is," he said with a wry smile and a wink.

I told Wild Bill how he was responsible for my losing Maggie, and he allowed as he hardly knew the girl — never said a word to her outside of what it took from time to time to conduct business at Goldstein's store.

"Still and all," I said, "she took a shine to you and it got to be too much for me to handle, her fixation and all. When she begged me to let her see the bullet holes you put in Phil Coe, well, that was the end of it so far as I was concerned. Broke my heart, all but. Still, I had to get away from there. And her. And you."

Hickok mulled that over for a while, and again said he hardly knew the girl and did nothing to encourage her fascination.

Then, "Son, I ain't never had no inkling as to the ways of womenfolk. I have scouted and I have tracked and I have guided and could follow the trail I was looking for more often than not. Hell, I can track the path of a prairie falcon that crossed an empty sky two days gone.

"But when it comes to women, they don't leave no trace that I can see. And without you know where they've been, you can't fathom where they're a-goin'. So don't expect me to shed any light on what got into that red-headed lass."

We sat in silence for a time. Then Wild Bill asked about the undertaking business, and I told him how I wasn't in that line of work at present, instead supplying coffins to undertakers around the city.

"Not injecting that stuff into the dead anymore, then?"

I shook my head. "No. I may go back to it. But for now, the appeal isn't there."

"Kind of how I feel about totin' a badge. After that affair in Abilene, I'll leave enforcing the law up to others. 'Course had I been here last night, circumstances may have required my lending a hand. Lord knows the Kansas City police wasn't worth much."

"What happened last night?"

"Why, haven't you heard, son? Place got robbed. In broad daylight — well, the sun was goin' down but it was still plenty of light, I'm told. Seems three yahoos with masks over their faces rode up to the Twelfth Street Gate easy as you please. Two of them pulled their pistols and burned a little powder to scare folks. The other one of 'em climbed off his horse and pointed a gun at the man in the ticket booth, then reached in and grabbed the cash box. He mounted up and they threw a little more lead around, then rode off."

"Sounds like nobody got hurt, though."

"Nobody was killed. But with all the shootin' them boys did, a little girl got wounded in her leg. Thing is, never mind that the police at this here Exposition are as thick as fleas on a coyote, them boys got away slick. Had I been on hand, that sure as hell wouldn't be the case."

I asked if there was any idea about the identity of the robbers.

"Oh, hell yes. Don't nobody know for sure, but it's fairly certain they're part of a band of unrepentant secessionists been thieving around these parts for some time now. Two of them is said to be brothers —

John and Cole Younger — and the other a tin-pot rebel who fancies himself a bad man, name of Jesse James."

I wondered why the law couldn't arrest them if their identities were known. Wild Bill laughed.

"Hell, son, half the people hereabouts is on their side. Bunch of damn Confederates who won't believe the war's over. They hide them out, give them fresh horses, feed them and give them supplies. Even some of the newspapers write up that they are heroes and such. Ever I lay eyes on them, I will shoot them deader than hell."

As we finished off the last of our lemonade — which was no longer cold, given the length of our conversation — a band concert started up across the way.

"What say we go listen to the music, son." It wasn't a question.

The band had already attracted a big crowd by the time we arrived. Front and center in the throng was a clot of broad-brimmed Texas sombreros of a type commonplace in Abilene but which I rarely saw in Kansas City.

"You had best be careful," Wild Bill said with a twinkle in his eye. "Them cowboys see that hoof and dewclaws you're paradin' around on, they're likely to rope and brand you."

The remark surprised me, as he had not commented on the oddity of my steer-like peg leg before then. I wondered at the presence of the forty or fifty cowboys.

"Most likely heard about the big doin's and came in on a train from Newton or Wichita or wherever they took their herds. Even some from Abilene, maybe, if the town will allow cattle anymore. Said they wouldn't, but money talks."

After a few songs, when the applause following a number died down, one of the Texas cowboys fired his revolver in the air and hollered, "Play Dixie!"

His request started something of a ruction among his cohorts. More pistols were drawn, more shots fired, and more shouts demanding the rebel anthem filled the air. The band leader looked reluctant, but when a cowboy propped his elbows on the edge of the bandstand and pointed a pair of revolvers at the conductor, he tapped the music stand with his baton, raised his arms, and, on the downbeat, the strains of "Dixie" started somewhat tentatively but soon took full voice. The cowboys cheered and accompanied the tune with occasional pistol shots.

With every note, I watched a crimson

flush climb higher up Wild Bill's neck. He walked with a purpose around the crowd, elbowed his way to the bandstand, and climbed the stairs. Taking the conductor gently by the elbow, he whispered something to the man. The bandleader shook his head and kept time despite Hickok's hand on his elbow.

Even from a distance, I watched Wild Bill's knuckles whiten as his grip tightened and he said, louder this time, "Stop playing."

Seeing the look in Wild Bill's eyes, the conductor stopped beating time and the music stopped in a cascade of discordant notes as the instruments fell silent in turn.

"Thank you," Hickok said. "I cannot stomach that song."

He turned to the crowd to see the bores in the barrels of some fifty revolvers fixed upon his person. He said not a word. He swept aside the front sides of his coat to reveal his twin revolvers and rested his hands on their butts.

Then he fixed his gaze on one after another of the Texas cowboys, as if daring any one — or all — of them to challenge him. No one took up the challenge and after a few tense moments you could hear the sound of pistols sliding into their holsters.

The cowboys whispered and milled around and finally made their way through the crowd and headed for the Exhibition exit like one of their driven herds.

I never saw Wild Bill Hickok in Kansas City after that day. But I had a feeling our trails would intersect again.

CHAPTER EIGHT

The drummer from Dubuque fanned his hand back and forth, wafting the clouds of steam rising from the serving dishes the landlady dropped on the table.

"Miz Morgan, it would be a certain pleasure if you would lay some kindling in that stove in the corner and strike a match to it. This room is an icebox."

Hannah Morgan, on her way out of the room to fetch the remainder of the meal, halted and with the sleeve of her housedress wiped sweat from her forehead. "I'll say only this, Mister Harvey: I am all but baked to a crisp from the heat in my kitchen. The milder temperature in the dining room is a welcome respite. Besides which, it makes little sense to waste wood warming a room used only twice a day for the taking of meals. Button your coat."

She said nothing more upon her return to the table, but the plate of steaming yeast rolls hit the table with a bit more force than necessary.

"This pot roast is perfection, Miz Morgan," I said after swallowing a forkful of the tender meat.

"Why thank you, Mister Collins. Beef is plentiful in Kansas City, but heaven knows the price of a good joint of meat comes dear."

The drummer, Arnold Harvey, stifled a belch. "Carrots are a mite underdone," he said, reaching for a roll.

"I declare, Mister Harvey, you are a hard man to please. Impossible, even. It is an unsolved mystery to me why you keep coming back here."

Sopping his torn bread roll in the meat juices on his plate, Harvey said, "I often wonder myself, Miz Morgan. I suspect the memories fade as I travel elsewhere."

"You should take a lesson from Mister Collins, here. He never complains. Or you could take advice from the Good Book. 'Having food and raiment let us be therewith content,' it says somewhere. One of the Timothies, if I am not mistaken."

"What do you have to say, Collins?" Harvey waggled his fork in my direction. When I answered with only a shrug and kept eating, he stifled a belch and said, "Say, how's about you put that soup bone you wear for a leg to work and mosey down to the alehouse with me for a drink when you're finished with your supper? I know a place."

I considered the offer, deciding an evening away from the boardinghouse would be a welcome diversion. The winter seemed to have dragged on endlessly and the long hours working in the shed, bundled up with a book in the parlor, or tossing and turning in bed were wearing on me.

I nodded my acceptance, finished off the bitter dregs in my coffee mug, and pushed my empty plate away with a thank you to Miz Morgan. I should not have bothered changing out of my working trousers before we left, as the cuffs of my clean pair were soon sodden and muddy from slogging through the mucky late-winter streets of Kansas City.

"Call me Arnold — or Arnie," the drummer said as we entered the tavern. While we had talked over meals at the boardinghouse during his visits there and our chats had been congenial, never before had he shown such familiarity. We stepped up to the bar and the bartender set aside the glass he was polishing and tossed the towel over his shoulder. I asked for a beer.

"It's the fruit of the vine for me," Arnie

said. "Give me a glass of your finest wine — make that the bottle, if you will."

So hazy and fly-specked was the mirrored back bar that it barely reflected the bottles on display. Elbows and sleeves had long since buffed the finish off the bar itself, leaving the wood splotched and sticky. Even in the dim light, water stains on the wallpaper were evident, as were discolored splotches and patches of flaky rust on the pressed-tin ceiling from a sometime leaky roof. But the place was warm and cozy, and offered a respite from the rooming house. It was quiet, too. A pair of old men shifted dominoes at one table as three others stood by watching. The only other patron leaned against the far end of the bar watching us, but I paid him no attention.

We carried our drinks to a table against the far wall, near enough to feel the effects of a woodstove, but not uncomfortably close. Arnie poured and emptied a glass of wine and refilled his glass in the time it took me to test the temperature of my beer.

"Mister Harvey — Arnie — I know you are in sales and travel a good deal, and that you are from Iowa, but that is all I know. What is your line?"

"Notions, primarily. You know the thing — buttons, snaps, hooks and eyes, pins and pin cushions, collar stays, seam rippers, measuring tapes, sewing chalk. I sell to general merchandise and dry goods stores for the most part. Some to dressmakers and tailors and seamstresses. Lately I've taken on a new line of home sewing machines. If you were at the Exposition last fall, you may have seen the Beckwith Portable Sewing Machine."

Arnie smiled and launched into his spiel. "Ten dollars only, the price — less than half the cost of other home sewing machines. For the money, the buyer gets the machine, hemmer, guide, bottle of oil, and four needles."

I dragged an empty chair away from the table and hoisted my peg leg onto the seat. A long day standing in the shop and the walk here had tired my hip and thigh, as well as settling a dull ache in my lower back. Arnie ignored the disturbance and talked on.

"Collins, this little beauty of a sewing machine clamps right on the edge of the table. Runs by a crank, which operates a hinged bar that raises and lowers the needle and thread as it pulls the fabric along. You might think a sewing machine at this price would be shoddy, but no. As the advertisements say, the Beckwith sewing machine is practical, durable, simple, and beautiful. The entire machine is richly plated. Could anyone be surprised it has fast become a popular favorite?"

Unsure as to whether the question was rhetorical of if he wanted an answer, I took a sip of my beer rather than respond. I looked around the room, noticed the man at the end of the bar still watching us. I studied the watcher as Arnie reeled off his usual route through his territory.

"Dubuque, Cedar Rapids, Des Moines, Saint Joseph . . ."

The watcher was a young man, too young, perhaps, to frequent a drinking establishment. A big lad, he was, but a lad nonetheless — I pegged him at sixteen, or perhaps seventeen, years of age.

"Kansas City, Lawrence, Topeka, Manhattan, Salina . . ."

From his dress, the young man looked to be a farmer. Given his age, most likely still in the employ of his father. His clothing, patched but clean, barely fit him so it seemed he had yet to get his growth. His scuffed-up brogans, too, were patched and stitched.

"Denver, Cheyenne, North Platte, Grand Island, Lincoln . . ."

The boy drained off a glass of whiskey as

I watched, and from his demeanor I thought it not his first. Nor would it be his last. I imagined he'd been sent to the city on an errand of some sort, and used the visit to sample its forbidden delights.

"Omaha, Des Moines again, then back home to Dubuque. Now, then. That's what I do, Collins. I haven't talked so much without selling something in quite a spell. So suppose you tell me what it is you do all day out there in Hannah Morgan's shed."

I turned away from the boy, but his gaze remained riveted on me and Arnie. Arnie's eyes widened when I told him I made coffins.

"It's many a man I have met in my travels, but never have I encountered one in your line of work."

"It is an unusual trade," I said. "Not one usually practiced on its own. Oftentimes furniture or cabinet makers have it as a sideline. In a city of this size, I find enough work. Smaller towns, though, undertakers are often on their own and must learn to fashion their own boxes. I knew something of woodworking as my pa made furniture back in Kentucky — he was a farmer, really, but liked to work with wood of an evening and in the winter months. Learned to handle tools helping him. But I came by

85

coffin making through working as an undertaker."

"Undertaker? You mean to tell me you are an undertaker?"

"By trade. But I am not in the business at present. I just provide 'eternity boxes' for other embalmers."

Arnie splashed wine on the table in an attempt to refill his glass.

"I am getting a little stir crazy of late. Might go back to undertaking. But I'll have to leave here to do it. Go west somewhere, out to where it isn't so settled, and set up shop in a growing town. That's what I did in Abilene."

"Damn. I cannot imagine why anyone would do such work."

"Really?" I watched Arnie squirm and shudder. "You know, Arnie, that we all cross the Jordan sooner or later. What would you have done with all the dead bodies? Leave them where they lie?"

Before Arnie could offer an answer, a shadow fell over the table.

"Hey, mister," the farm boy said. "What the hell is that?"

I looked up at the boy and followed his gaze down his arm to a pointed finger and beyond to my wooden leg, propped on the seat of the chair.

Arnie said, "Hey, hayseed, mind your own business!"

"This don't concern you none, mister. You best just shut your mouth."

"It's all right, Arnie," I said. Then, to the boy, "What does it look like to you?"

"Looks like a cow's leg. Anybody can see that. What I mean is, why you wearin' a wooden cow leg?"

I didn't answer, just watched the inebriated farm boy weave slowly back and forth. A long minute or so later, he raised a foot, placed it after a couple of tries to a rail on the chair and pushed it aside.

My peg leg hit the floor with a clunk loud enough to draw the attention of the barkeep, the domino players, and their onlookers.

"I asked you a question, mister."

"You're drunk, young man. Go back to the bar. Better still, go sleep it off."

"Not 'fore I get an answer."

"Listen, boy, you're causing a disturbance. Now, go away."

"Who you callin' a boy?" he hollered, yanking off his cloth cap and swinging it at me.

I ducked away, the cap missed its mark, and the momentum of the swing staggered the boy. I grabbed the edge of the table and was on my feet faster than he could regain his. He turned toward me and with both hands reset the cap on his head and pulled it snug.

"You're in a heap of trouble now, mister."

"Go away. I'll not tell you again."

"You ain't tellin' me nothin', you city slicker." He raised his fists. "You're about to get a whippin'."

I saw the jab coming and jerked my head aside as it flew past, striking nothing but air. The boy stumbled, but regained his balance and launched a haymaker from near the floor. It, too was easily dodged. The boy lurched past in the wake of the swing, and as he did, I swung my peg leg into his path and swept his legs from under him. He hit the floor face first with no attempt to break his fall.

He took a deep breath, attempted to get his arms under himself and raise up, but managed only an inch or two before dropping again. I gave myself a moment to catch my breath, then reached down and grabbed an arm below the shoulder and rolled the boy over. His nose streamed blood and if his eyes were focused on anything, it was nothing in this world.

Arnie, still seated at the table, tossed the wine in his glass onto the boy's face. He snorted, sputtered, blinked, and looked around. He came to himself and remembered where he was. His eyes locked on mine and he hiked himself up on his elbows in an attempt to sit up.

Instead, he found himself flat on the floor again, this time with the hoof of my wooden leg pressed to his throat.

"Just stay put. I don't want to hurt you."

He sneered and tried again to rise, only to succumb to the pressure of my weight as I pressed down on the peg leg. One more try to rise brought the same result and he wilted.

"All right, mister," he said, tears mixing with the blood and wine on his face.

"You'll leave off if I let you up?"

He nodded, I swung the wooden leg aside, reached out a hand, and pulled him to his feet. More unsteady than ever, he quickly sat on the chair he had earlier kicked aside. The bartender was there with a towel and a cup of steaming coffee.

"Here you go, kid. Drink this, clean yourself up, and get the hell out of here. Don't need your kind in here causing trouble."

The fight — if a fight it can be called — seemed to have sobered the boy up some.

"I'm awful sorry. Don't know what that drink done to me. Ain't used to the stuff."

He turned to me. "Sorry to you, as well, sir. I was just curious, mostly. Forgot my manners. Lost my temper. I don't know."

"No harm done. If I was you, I'd lay off the whiskey."

"Yessir."

I sat down in my chair and hiked up the pant leg over my peg leg. "What it is, is a wooden leg. Got my foot shot off by a cannonball in the war and the doc cut off some more of my leg. They did a lot of that, then. Arms. Legs."

The boy looked on in wonder.

"And so I've got this peg leg so I can walk more or less like a normal person."

"But why does it look like a cow leg?"

I laughed. "No reason. No reason at all. Just for the hell of it, I guess. A man has to get around on a stump of wood, he might just as well have some fun with it." I pulled the pant leg back down. "Satisfied?"

The boy nodded, then hung his head.

"Arnie, I'm for getting back to Miz Hannah Morgan's boardinghouse. What do you say?"

CHAPTER NINE

When Arnold Harvey next arrived in Kansas City, spring had preceded him by several weeks; perhaps as much as a month. A knock on the door disturbed my work, and I wondered who the rare visitor might be.

"Arnie! Back in town, I see."

"Indeed. Not been in any bar fights since I was last here, I trust."

"Not a one. My rowdy behavior seems to be limited to drinking bouts in your company."

Harvey looked around the shed, mostly empty now. The clean and empty workbench, small stack of lumber against the far wall, and three finished coffins propped against the wall beside the door did not speak to a thriving enterprise. Even the sawdust and wood shavings that usually carpeted the floor had been swept up and burned in the pot-bellied stove, now cold.

"Ol' Hannah Morgan said you were out

here. Thought I'd stick my nose in. Hope you don't mind. Got to thinking I'd never been out here."

I shooed Arnie toward the stool at the bench. "Not at all. Come in," I said, then slid one of the boxes down from the wall and sat myself on its lid.

"If I didn't know better, I'd say you were moving out. Where are your tools and equipment and such?"

"All packed up." I nodded toward the heavy canvas bag under the bench. "Hannah didn't tell you then?"

Arnie shook his head.

I reached into my pocket and handed him one of the new calling cards I'd had made up by a local printer. JONATHON 'PINEBOX' COLLINS, it read. EMBALMER & UNDERTAKER. "I am leaving Kansas City."

"But why?" he said as he studied the card.

I mulled over the best way to frame a reply. "You didn't hear what happened here last week?"

Arnie's curious look said he had not.

I adjusted my seat on the box, hoisted my "hoof" onto the opposite knee and said, "Well, I was here working that afternoon — ordinary kind of day it was, clouds threatening a storm. Started in to raining, then something went 'thunk' on the roof. Then, after a bit, a 'clunk' and another, then another. Too noisy for raindrops, if you know what I mean. Stuck my head out to see what was up. Now, you will not believe this, Arnie, but it was frogs."

"Frogs?"

"As sure as we are both sitting here. Frogs, falling from the sky. They were landing 'splat' and 'plop' all over the ground — that was what I heard hitting the roof. It was raining frogs in Kansas City."

I don't know if Arnie looked more shocked or skeptical.

"On my honor, Arnie. Ask Miz Morgan. Ask around town. It was in the newspapers and all. I'm surprised you didn't read about it."

Arnie shook his head in wonder, brow furrowed in uncertainty. He mulled it over for a minute, looked to cast the thought aside, then said, "What's that got to do with you leaving?"

"A biblical plague of frogs. Like with Moses. On account of Kansas City being such a hotbed of sin and iniquity. That's what Miz Morgan says. She's expecting lice and boils and locusts any day now. I decided I had best get away before it comes down to the deaths of the firstborn."

You hear about people's jaws dropping in

surprise, but you seldom see it. But that is what happened with Arnie. Then he started working his jaw in search of words. He looked troubled. And confused. "You can't mean it, Collins. Surely you don't believe that."

I let him stew for a time before I laughed. "Of course not, Arnie. It did rain frogs, mind you, but I don't expect any more plagues to befall us."

It was merely an itch to move on, I told him, pointing out that as a traveling sales-man he should understand more than most the need for a change in scenery. He allowed as how that was so, and asked where I was bound for.

"West," I said. I explained that, having decided to get back into The Dismal Trade, I needed a smaller town without much established competition, but with prospects to grow quickly and provide enough clien-tele to allow an undertaking business to thrive. A situation, I said, much like what I had encountered in Abilene.

"But," I said, "I have had my fill of cow towns. I have decided to try a mining district. There is a silver boom out in Nevada at a place called Pioche. I have been reading about it in the papers, and I believe it fills the bill."

"Nevada, eh? Never been out there myself. Haven't been any farther west than Denver, or Cheyenne. But I hear tell them mining towns are pretty rough."

"Can't be much more so than a place like Abilene when a herd of Texas cowboys hits town."

Arnie stood and grasped my shoulder. "Well, you're a young man. Don't suppose you can go too wrong. If it don't work out, you can always come back to civilization and start again. When you leaving?"

"In the morning. There's a dray coming by later to haul my trunk and tools and such to the train station."

"We had best have a drink this evening, then, so I can offer up a toast to safe travel."

"Last time I went for a drink with you I nearly got thrashed. I appreciate the offer, but there's too much still to do. We'll clink coffee mugs at Miz Morgan's supper."

I stepped off the train in Palisades, Nevada, to the sound of gunfire. People were rushing around the street, dogs barked, horses panicked, and masked bandits shot their way out of a small frame building with BANK painted on its false front.

Sidling behind a stack of crates on the boardwalk beside the small train station, I

95

watched the turmoil. The locomotive whistle sounded and the train puffed its way out of town and, as if on cue, firearms found their holsters, the outlaws pulled down their masks, women and children ceased running about, and one and all gathered in the middle of the street, laughing and talking. I learned later that it was all a sham — repeated with every train, so passengers passing through would remember the town. To think it would lure them back — as seemed to be the purpose of the play-acting — struck me as absurd, but who is to say.

Nevada is not close to anywhere. And when you get there, there's a distinct feeling that you are nowhere. From Kansas City, I had made connections to the transcontinental rail and, save a few brief stops to bolt down a greasy, gelatinous diner meal, my days and nights were a monotony of clickety-clacking wheels as the train rocked and swayed its way across boundless plains, over and around never-ending mountains, and through endless canyons.

Palisades took its name from the sheer stone walls of one such defile, Ten Mile Canyon. The burg was home to only a few hundred people, but business in the town was brisk as it was the main supply station for mining districts nearly three hundred miles to the south, including the diggings around Pioche.

Parades of freight wagons plied the road, hauling mining equipment, along with most everything else the isolated town needed to support itself. Stagecoaches raced one another up and down the trail, carrying express boxes and passengers — experienced and would-be miners, salesmen, gamblers, assayers, millworkers, cooks, lawyers, engineers, storekeepers, bartenders, store clerks, mine executives, and every other kind of able-bodied man chasing the next big chance.

Missing, for the most part, were females. I would learn that Pioche suffered, at present, a painful shortage of women, to the point that saloon girls could command a price just for walking among the men. It was a scarcity that would be cured in time, but not necessarily with the kind of feminine influence that tends to tame a town.

I noticed another kind of passenger boarding the coaches — men with the look of toughs and gunfighters, hoodlums and desperados. I had seen their kind in Springfield, in Abilene, even in Kansas City. But if their numbers on the road to Pioche were representative of their presence in the town, I questioned my choice of destination.

Despite daily runs to Pioche, I waited three days in Palisades for a seat on the overburdened stage line. I kept back only a grip with a few essentials; my trunk and tool bag I sent on ahead on a fast freight wagon. Even so, I would likely arrive a couple of days ahead of it in a faster six-horse coach.

When the time finally came to board the stage, the driver checked tickets and assembled the full-fare passengers into a group. Of note among us was a young woman — accompanied by a young man I assumed to be her husband. Their dress and appearance marked them as city folks of some means — she in a frilly dress and packing a lacy parasol, him stiff and starched from shined shoes to bowler hat. One man reminded me of the professional gamblers who frequented the saloons in Abilene, three other men looked to be business types, another was a working man, and there was another who had the look of a gunman.

The shotgun guard and station agent filled the front and rear boots with an express box, mail bags, and as many passenger bags as would fit. The rest were lashed to the roof of the coach.

"Looks like we got room for four up top," the driver said to the men standing by in hopes of a ride. "Who's first?"

The station agents checked their tickets and assembled the four with priority. Those disappointed muttered and wandered away. One of the chosen four, another likely gunslinger to my mind, sidled over to the working man in our group. "Le'me see that ticket," the tough said. The working man, who looked to be a year or two younger than me, stepped back, puzzled.

"Let's see it," the weathered ruffian said in a voice as flat and hard as his stare.

The young man held forth the ticket with trembling hand.

"Just as I thought. There's been a mistake."

"Wh-what? That can't be. I bought that ticket my ownself. Been in my pocket ever since."

Placing a hand atop the pistol strapped to his waist, the man said, "I'm tellin' you there's been a mix-up. This here ticket's mine." He pointed toward the top of the coach with his chin. "You're ridin' up there, boy."

"But —"

"Ain't no buts about it. Unless, that is, you aim to make trouble here."

"I — I —" The worker cut short his response when the gun, no longer holstered, was pressed into his gut.

Like me, a few of our fellow passengers witnessed the altercation, including the woman. Most chose to ignore it, and neither the driver, guard, nor agent appeared to have noticed, being otherwise occupied with readying the coach and teams.

The gunman holstered his revolver and, one by one, met the gaze of those of us who witnessed the set-to. In the meantime, the other passenger with the look of a desperado came to stand beside him, adding his intimidation to the mix.

"Any objections from you-all?"

No one, myself included I am sorry to say, spoke a word.

"Gather 'round," the driver said, cutting the tension. "There's a few things you ought to know. There ain't a whole hell of a lot — excuse my language, ma'am," he said with a nod toward the lone female passenger. "My language tends to get a mite coarse now and then, on account of these horses don't understand any other kind of talk. Anyway, as I was saying, there ain't much between here and where we're a-going. The stage stations along the way are rude affairs, and the food, what there is of it, ain't nothing to boast about. Stops will be as quick as we can make them, so do your business in a hurry, if you have any.

"The road is well traveled, but that don't mean it's any good. There's as many rocks as there is road, and more chuckholes than both, and you'll feel every one of them. It's mountainous country, and some of it's steep. You'll be asked now and again to get out and walk up the hills to save the horses, and it ain't no request — you will get out and walk. That includes you, ma'am," he said with a nod to the woman.

"If you nod off, don't use whoever's sittin' next to you for a pillow. If you're inclined to smoke or spit, make damn sure to do it so's it don't blow back through the windows. When it gets too dusty — and it will — pull down the curtains for as long as you can stand it or till the air's all used up. If I was you, young feller," he said, pointing his whipstock at the man accompanying the woman, "I'd pull that chamber pot you're wearin' for a hat down snug, 'cause that bear grease in your hair will attract dust like flies to a gut pile."

When the chuckles subsided, the driver talked on. "We don't expect no trouble, but it's best if you stay alert. These stagecoaches get robbed from time to time, and the bandits don't care if we're comin' or goin'. The crooks seem to know when a coach is packin' a payroll, which we ain't — but that don't mean they won't stop us anyway. Paiutes ain't been troublesome lately, but you never know. They ain't none too pleased with all of us over-running their country."

The driver looked us over. Looked up at the shotgun guard, already in his seat, who nodded at him. "Any questions? Good. All aboard, then. Let's get this show on the road."

CHAPTER TEN

It is altogether possible that riding in a cramped and crowded stagecoach offers a glimpse of the eternity faced by occupants of coffins I have built.

Pressed from every direction, even the slightest movement is difficult. The air is stifling and in short supply. And there is no relief from the unpleasant odors that curdle and congeal. The only difference, perhaps, is the presence of light and sight. And with every mile, I thanked luck or good fortune or God above that I was seated opposite the young woman. The view was much to be desired, particularly when compared to the alternatives.

The woman, offered first choice of seats when boarding, chose the left side of the front seat, facing rearward; her husband next to her in the center. I faced forward on the center bench, on the left side of the coach opposite the woman.

Next to me sat a traveling salesman, and, like Arnie and many in his line of work, he owned the gift of gab. It was not long into the trip until he struck up a conversation, his incessant questions and probing queries revealing more, perhaps, than his fellow passengers wished to either reveal or know. He started with the dapper young couple across from him. Coming west from Chicago, the man was a lawyer, trading on a few years' experience with a big-city law firm for a position with a mining syndicate.

The salesman said, "What is it you will be doing in Pioche?"

"Sorting out discrepancies and disagreements over mining claims," the lawyer said.

That drew a laugh from the coarse-looking man next to the salesman. While he shared the center bench with us, he sat facing to the rear, opposite his likewise tough-looking companion. The seating arrangement facilitated their passing back and forth a bottle of whiskey, from which they drank directly. As stagecoach manners require, they offered the bottle all around. There were no takers.

Wiping away the laugh — and the remnants of whiskey — with the sleeve of his jacket, he said, "Looks like you and me are in the same line of work." He waved the whiskey bottle in the direction of his drinking buddy. "Lonigan here and me, we been hired by a mining company to do the same thing as you." He laughed again, took another drink from the bottle, and handed it to Lonigan. "But I suspect we'll go about settlin' them disputes in a different way." Lonigan, too, laughed, then tipped back the bottle for a long drink.

The lawyer squirmed in his seat, took his wife's hand in his own, and gave it a reassuring pat. "What is your line?" he asked the salesman.

"Explosives. High explosives. Our firm is opening markets in mining districts across the country."

The man seated in the corner next to the lawyer, who spent most of his time dozing — or pretending to — perked up with the revelation. "High explosives, you say? Nitroglycerin, you mean?"

"No, sir. Although we offer nitro, we do not recommend it owing to its volatility. We also offer black powder, of course, despite its relative inefficiency. What is your interest, if I might ask?"

"I am a mine engineer. Work for the Meadow Valley Mining Company in Pioche."

The salesman smiled. "Ah, yes. Meadow Valley. Your firm is at the top of my list of prospects."

"If not nitroglycerin, then, you must be talking dynamite."

Again, the salesman smiled. "Indeed I am. You are familiar with it?"

The mining engineer sat up straighter in his seat. "Some. I believe you will find a ready market. The black powder we — and the other mines — use is too bulky. Storing it is a pain. A few months back, September it was, a bunch of Mexican miners was celebrating Independence Day where they come from. The party got out of hand, I guess, and a fire started in the cantina where the festivities were. Burned down a bunch of the main street.

"Then it hit Felsenthal's store. Place was built out of stone; said to be fireproof. But there was three hundred or so barrels of blasting powder in the basement. Blew the whole place sky high. Hell, there was a vault door weighed half a ton that landed clear out of town. The explosion and all the rubbish it sent flying killed thirteen folks. Spread fire everywhere, too. Near burnt down the whole damn town."

The lawyer said, "An interesting story, sir. But I'll ask you to watch your language. Keep in mind there is a lady present."

The toughs laughed. But the engineer,

face red, leaned forward in his seat and tipped his hat to the lawyer's wife. "I beg your pardon, ma'am. Spent so much time in the mines I forget myself sometimes. That, and the company of women is something I don't enjoy much — often, I mean."

A smile was all it took to signal the woman's forgiveness.

"Has the town been rebuilt?" I asked the engineer.

"Some," he said, relieved at the shift in conversation. "But they can't freight lumber in fast enough. There's buildings cobbled together from salvaged boards, some of the businesses with stone walls have been repaired. But there's still a lot of canvas over folks' heads in Pioche."

The conversation continued around the coach. We heard from the miner in the rear corner. Failing to find his fortune at various times and places from the Park City mines in Utah Territory, to Butte and Bannack in Montana Territory, to Leadville in Colorado, he thought to try his luck in Pioche.

"You'll have no trouble finding work," the engineer advised. "But if you're planning to prospect on your own, you'll be buttin' heads with established mines and they won't take kindly to it."

The gambler on the rear seat was even

more well-traveled than the miner, telling of having plied his trade on Mississippi riverboats, in cow-town saloons, mining camps, and cities and towns up and down and across the western half of the country. After that brief introduction, he had little else to say, and the "poker face" he likely employed at the tables served him as well in the stagecoach. The gunmen said nothing more of themselves, and contributed little to the conversation save a snide remark from time to time or rude laughter at moments that seemed inappropriate.

Conversation waxed and waned through the day and into the night with some hours of quiet in the dead of night. With the rocking of the coach on its thoroughbraces, some of our seatmates managed to doze deep enough to work up a snore, but those of us on the center bench, having no backrest, could do little but hang on to the ceiling straps and nod off occasionally, only to snap back to wakefulness when the coach hit a rock or chuckhole.

After an early morning stop to switch teams, with a few minutes to stretch our legs, visit the backhouse, and stave off hunger with lukewarm porridge and hot coffee, it was back on the road. The topside riders, like the driver and shotgun guard, were hardly recognizable, coated as they were with a thick film of dust clinging to clothing, skin, hair, and hat alike. Application of wash water helped but a little, serving mostly to turn the dust to mud.

Having said little of myself during yesterday's introductions and conversations beyond the usual explanations about my missing leg and the peg leg that replaced it, curiosity about me naturally led to inquiries once we were back on the road, rocking our way toward Pioche. I confess that I, myself, struck up the band when I asked the engineer — the only one among us with first-hand knowledge of Pioche — about the likelihood of finding a small commercial building to rent. Although I anticipated his answer based on his description of the fire, I could not help but feel crestfallen. With businesses of all sorts vying for space and building materials and labor, the city was bursting at the seams and unable to keep up with the growth.

The salesman released a barrage of questions. "Where is it you're coming from? Were you in business there? You looking to do the same in Pioche? What line of work are you in, anyway?"

I told that I had come out from Kansas City and that, yes, I had a small business there but was looking for a fresh start.

The explosives peddler was relentless. "Sure. But what is it you do?"

Seeing no reason not to own up to my chosen field, I fished around in a pocket for my business cards. "Of late, I have been building coffins. Fact is, I have turned out coffins for some years now. That's all I did in Kansas City, but before that, in Abilene, it was a sideline of sorts to my main trade." With that, I dealt cards to the salesman, the lawyer, and the mine engineer. I turned in my seat and passed some to the gambler, who passed cards to the miner and the two toughs.

It was no surprise to me that the card stifled conversation. My fellow passengers looked at the card, looked at me, and then back at the card, which they studied as intently as if it contained the entire text of the Chicago City Directory rather than simply JONATHON 'PINEBOX' COLLINS, EMBALMER & UNDERTAKER.

Just before the tension boiled over, the gunman across the coach laughed. Just a chuckle at first, then boisterously, as though riding in a stagecoach with an undertaker was the most amusing thing that had ever happened. His companion joined in, but his hilarity lacked sincerity.

When his laughter turned to a coughing fit, and the coughing subsided, the gunslinger wiped his mouth and eyes with his shirtsleeve and said, "So you're a wormfood farmer? I'll be damned! Could be I'll be sendin' some business your way. Don't suppose you'd consider givin' me and Lonigan here a cut of your profits for any corpses we supply?"

The question launched another bout of amusement among the gunmen, but only contributed to the uncomfortable silence of the other passengers. With talk at a standstill, I opened *The Moonstone* to the dog-eared page I had marked and amused myself with Wilke Collins's detective novel as we rocked along.

To say we were all tired and irritable when finally reaching Pioche would be an understatement. But no sooner had the driver reined up the teams in front of the stage line office on the main street than we were jarred fully awake.

At first, I thought the gunplay in the street was all for show, all play-acting, as it had been in Palisades. But that thought lasted only as long as it took for a bullet to smash through the door panel next to me and into the frame of the seat beneath me.

All was confusion and panic as the up-top passengers scrambled down the protected side of the coach. The gunfighter across the coach drew his revolver and jumped out the opposite door with his cohort on his heels. The mine engineer, salesman, and gambler clogged the opening as each struggled to get through ahead of the others. The miner on the backseat slid across, arms wrapped around his head, which was tucked between his knees.

I stole a glance at the lawyer and his wife. Both were immobile, pale-faced and trans-fixed on the shootout just feet away. Another stray bullet whistled through my window, drilling a hole in the padding of the seat back mere inches above the ducked-down miner. I chanced a look out the window and saw a bullet rip the lower jaw off a man holding a smoking gun, which he dropped. He crumpled to the dusty street, gushing blood. Another man lay near where he fell, this one with two — maybe more — bloody holes in his shirtfront and blood staining the shredded fabric on the thigh of a shot-up leg. Through the haze of dust and gun smoke, a third man fell, too far away for me to see where he'd been shot.

The gunfire stopped as suddenly as it had started. The lawyer and his wife had not moved an inch. For that matter, neither had I. The woman trembled. Her husband wrapped his arm around her shoulder, but she resisted his attempts to pull her close. Our loud-mouthed gunfighter's face loomed in the opposite window and his laugh — by now familiar, but still grating — filled the coach.

"Well folks," he said, "welcome to Pioche. Looks like you got some customers already, Mister Pinebox Collins."

CHAPTER ELEVEN

I looked on as the smoke cleared and the dust settled. Traffic on the main street of Pioche soon returned to normal — the wagons and carriages and horses and those afoot dodging the bodies. A lawman and deputy looked things over and talked with the surviving gunfighters and a few witnesses. Apparently deciding the shootings — whatever the cause — were justified, they waved away the detained people. The marshal, or county sheriff, or whatever authority the man held, walked off, leaving the deputy to keep an eye on things until the bodies were removed. I stood by, grip in hand, waiting to see who would haul away the dead, thinking it might provide the opportunity for an introduction to the undertaking business in Pioche.

Loud voices from the stagecoach drew my attention. The lawyer stood on the street leaning in through the door of the coach. I could hear his wife's voice — seldom heard on the road to here, and certainly not at this volume — coming from inside. Curious, but not wanting to interfere, I stepped off the boardwalk and eased my way around to stand on the street side where I could overhear the argument unseen.

The woman allowed at some length that Pioche was crude and uncivilized, and she had no intention of settling here.

The lawyer, in an attempt to stay calm, reminded her of his job here — that he had accepted employment with the mining company and the work necessitated his being here.

"I do not care a fig about mines or jobs or work. I cannot, will not, so much as set foot on the streets of such a barbaric place. Men shot down in broad daylight before my very eyes! I am telling you I will not have it!"

"Come along, dear. You're tired. We'll find our rooms at the hotel and rest. Things will look better once you are rested."

"Not a chance! And do not 'dear' me! I am not getting out of this stagecoach. You will have the man put my baggage back aboard and arrange return passage. After another interminable ride on this infernal conveyance I will board a train back to Chicago and civilization."

The lawyer sighed. "Need I remind you that our house in Chicago has been sold?"

"I do not care. Mummy and Father will welcome me. I shall live with them until you give up this ridiculous notion of working in this wasteland and return home!"

The argument continued as the hostlers hitched fresh teams to the Concord coach. With the arrival of an undertaker and what I took to be his young assistant pulling a handcart, I hurried into the stage line office and stowed my carpetbag, intending to follow the undertaker to his place of business.

I cannot say with any certainty what happened to the lawyer's wife. But I can say for sure she was never seen again in Pioche. Which is a shame, as the city would have surely benefited from the presence of one so lovely and charming. On the other hand, it is unlikely her influence — and that of a hundred more like her — could or would have turned back the stampede of violence and crudity.

I followed the handcart, pulled by the youngster and pushed by the undertaker up the hill past several streets, then off onto a side street, around a corner, and into an alley. This part of town looked to have escaped the fire that still scarred much of the city. The men opened the back door of a small log building and I watched as they hauled the bodies of the three dead gunfighters inside. I gave them a moment to get settled, then knocked at the front door. Above the frame, a small painted sign read, UNDER-TAKER, MARCUS HENRY, PROP.

The younger man answered my knock. I asked to see Mister Henry and he opened the door wide and walked away without a word, exiting the room through a door on the opposite wall. Assuming an invitation, I stepped inside and closed the door behind me. A small rolltop desk stood against a side wall, fronted by a table and two side chairs. Across the room, six identical chairs lined the walls in a U shape, focused on a long narrow table. The logs on the outer walls had been covered with lath and plaster and whitewash, with beadboard wainscoting painted white covering the bottom third of the walls. The door through which the young man exited the room penetrated the center of the back wall, flanked by two small tables, each holding a vase of wilted flowers. Red, flocked wallpaper covering the wall peeled away in places along the seams. Framed and faded lithographs of sylvan landscapes by European masters hung on the walls, seemingly at random. A small warming stove in the corner, with a battered coffeepot atop it, completed the furnishings.

Upon memorizing the room and all its contents, I sat in one of the chairs at the table near the desk and picked up a three-week-old newspaper from Salt Lake City and perused its pages. Somewhere in the middle of a Mormon harangue about ongoing difficulties with territorial officers sent out by the federal government, the inner door opened. In came Marcus Henry, wiping his hands on a towel stained with traces of blood.

"I am sorry to keep you waiting," he said as he walked around the table and sat in the wheeled desk chair. "I won't offer you my hand. I have been dealing with some bodies that just arrived. Victims of a gunfight," he said as he wiped between his fingers. "A messy business, this bunch."

"Yes, sir. I witnessed the melee. Hadn't even stepped off the stage when the shooting started."

"You're new in town, then."

I nodded and handed my card across the table. "You are Mister Henry, I presume."

He nodded and set the card on the table. "And you must be Jonathon 'Pinebox' Collins."

"I am, Mister Henry —"

"Please, call me Marc."

"Yes, sir, Marc. I have been living of late in Kansas City. I did not practice undertaking there. Instead, I set up shop providing coffins to the trade in the city."

"Why are you here?"

I shrugged. "Tired of Kansas City, I guess. Needed a change of air. The newspapers from time to time reported on the mining activities here, and it sounded like a good prospect — a growing place where I could set up shop and get established once again."

We talked about my experience in Abilene and Springfield, and my training and experience in Nashville. And I told him, of course, about my brief military service and the loss of my leg and the curious nature of my peg leg.

He told of how he had come west in 1849. His roughhewn features said he was now a man in his sixties. Or fifties. Even seventy would not be out of the question. The son of an undertaker, he abandoned his father and the establishment that was to be his in order to seek his fortune in the California goldfields. As for most who made the attempt, he said, gold mining proved a fickle mistress, and so, he turned back to undertaking.

"Laid out bodies in mining camps up and

down the Sierra, and in Sacramento for a while. Pulled up stakes and resettled up in the Comstock country. Virginia City." He waved around the room. "Most everything you see here is from there. Took my office apart and brought it with me — except the wallpaper. That," he said with a laugh, "came from an overambitious order by a woman opening up a brothel last year. Bought the remnants off her. Her place burned to the ground in the big fire. She stops by every now and then to look at the wallpaper and remember. Her place ain't so fancy these days, but she's sticking it out."

Henry — Marc — picked up my card, glanced at it, tapped the table with its edge. He leaned back in his chair and looked down his nose at me. "Not sure what you have in mind, young man. Was I you, I wouldn't plan on making a living building coffins. Pretty near every stick of wood you see in this town has to be freighted in. What ain't mine timber goes to them as is building houses and businesses. 'Bout the most anybody here can hope for is a standard six-board coffin. And that from green lumber, like as not. You'll find the business is different other ways, out here. On the frontier, so to speak."

He told how many, even most, of the men

in town were here on their own — no family, and no friends save those made here. With no one to care whether they lived or died, most burials were simple affairs and the undertaking the same. Funeral services were a rarity. Most bodies went into the grave with no one to witness their passing into eternal rest but the undertaker and the gravediggers. I asked about embalming.

"Don't know nothing about it, myself," he said. "Wasn't no such thing when I learned to lay out bodies back at my father's place. No call for it in the goldfields — most men died and was buried without ceremony. I suspect any families they had back where they come from had no notice of their passing.

"There was an undertaker in Virginia City who was a drainer. From knowing him, I know there was little call there for preserving bodies. Few got shipped out for burial, and them families as was burying one of their own in the town cemetery saw little need for it. Ain't much different here in Pioche. There's a place across town — Wilkinson and Nay — that will embalm a body if called upon. Me, like I said, wouldn't know the first thing about it. I don't expect it would be an easy job, as most of the bodies is all shot up like them we just brung in.

Fact is, there ain't a body buried here that died natural. Some got killed in the fire and explosion, some from accidents in the mines. Most of them died from gettin' shot."

This all proved to be true. By my count over the months to come, there were seventy-two people dead and buried in Pioche before a Bullionville millworker name of Mike Olsen succumbed to a case of consumption. All the rest died of violent means of one kind or another.

"I should like to talk more, Pinebox — I guess you don't mind being called that, beings as it's printed on your card — but, as you know, I have three bodies in the back needin' my attention."

I asked about the young man, assuming he was attending to the bodies.

Marcus laughed. "Dicky? Oh, he ain't no help. Not for laying out the dead, anyhow. Sad case, really, is our Dicky. Slab broke loose in the mine and a chunk of it knocked him on the head. Damn lucky it didn't kill him, but it did hurt him bad. Addled his brain somethin' fierce. He's simple-minded as a child, now. I call on him to help with liftin' and totin' and diggin' graves, that sort of thing. From his time in the mines, the boy sure knows how a shovel works — he can excavate a grave slick, even in this rocky soil. He makes enough money from me and some others who find a use for him to keep fed and clothed. I and them others kind of keep an eye out for Dicky. Keep folks with a mean streak from bothering him, if you know what I mean. He's a good lad."

With nothing to keep me from doing otherwise, I offered to help Marcus Henry prepare the dead gunfighters for the grave. Thus began my entrée into the undertaking business in Pioche, Nevada.

CHAPTER TWELVE

As quickly as Abilene had grown on the Kansas prairie, the Nevada desert mountainside where Pioche sprouted proved the more fertile ground. Stumping around the streets on my steer leg taught me the layout of the town. Raw lumber was everywhere, from the skeletons of buildings under construction to siding on those just finished. Paint, even whitewash, was a rarity, as was window glass. Canvas roofs and walls were commonplace in both business and residential districts. A few burned-out hulks remained from the big fire, but most of the lots were cleared, with new buildings built or underway.

The Pioche mines and mills never stopped working, day or night, as is the case with mines most everywhere. The streets of Pioche were as lively at four o'clock in the morning as they were at four o'clock in the afternoon. Ore wagons and freight wagons clogged the streets and roads, with the crack of whips and profane shouts of teamsters adding to a never-ending din. In my travels I counted seventy-one saloons, thirty-two brothels, three dance halls, and two theaters. The largest of the town's livery stables and wagon yards accommodated three hundred horses. There were, of course, a complement of dry goods stores and mercantiles, mining supply houses, banks and express offices, a firefighting company, a waterworks, and an apothecary.

And, of course, Pioche housed several gunsmiths whose shops repaired, refurbished, refitted, and even manufactured revolvers and long guns and supplied ammunition. The sound of gunfire was so commonplace it drew little notice — nor did the thump and whump and tremors resulting from blasting far underfoot in the drifts and stopes of the mines.

Marcus Henry provided enough work in assisting with his undertaking business and nailing up coffins to keep body and soul together, so to speak. But I had plenty of time for exploring the town and the surrounding mining district. I sometimes rented a carriage for my explorations outside the town, but more often than not the hostler at one of the smaller livery stables strapped my "stirrup" to a hired saddle and I went horseback. More than once on the paths and trails in the hills, men with drawn guns blocked my way, questioning my presence and threatening violence lest I reverse course.

One day, without notice, Marcus Henry took me on as a partner. Upon inserting my key in the front-door lock, a change in the signage caught my eye. His sign, rather than above the door, was affixed to the wall beside the door, even with the top of the frame. Below it was a perfect reproduction of my calling card: JONATHON 'PINEBOX' COLLINS, EMBALMER & UNDERTAKER.

"Marc!" I shouted as I flung open the door and stumped my way across the room, reaching the door to the back room just as Marcus Henry pulled it open.

"Yes?"

"The sign! You've put up a new sign!"

"Yes," he said with a nod.

"But why? This is most unexpected."

"Ain't you pleased with it? Did the sign painter misspell your name or something?"

"No, of course not."

"Then what is it?"

He watched for a time as I worked my jaw in an attempt to gnaw my thoughts into words. He said, "Sit down, Pinebox, before you fall down."

He led me by the elbow to one of the chairs facing the table in front of his desk. Rolling open the desk, he pulled a rolled-up oversize envelope from one of the cubbyholes. I watched as he shook out a sheaf of papers onto the tabletop and tapped their edges with his fingertips to align them in a tidy pile. He glanced at the top sheet, picked up the stack, tapped the bottom edge as if the papers needed further alignment, and passed them across to me.

I waded through the legalese as fast as I could, backtracking frequently to make sense of the lawyerly language. What it said, in essence, was that Marc was taking me into the business as a partner, offering ten percent ownership in the business and its profits, with a further ten percent transferred to me annually until we shared equal partnership of fifty percent each. The document also authorized me to make such improvements to the business, its services, fixtures, and furnishings with an eye to increased profitability as I saw fit. In the case of the demise of either of us, the surviving partner gained full title to the enterprise.

"I — I — I don't know what to say, Marc. This is most unexpected." I swallowed hard. "But, why?"

"Is it not to your liking?"

"No — yes — of course it is. As I said, it comes as a complete surprise."

Marc leaned forward in his chair, interlocking his fingers and placing the folded hands on the tabletop as I had seen him do numerous times when taking on a serious air in discussions with clients.

"You have more than proven your worth around here these past months. Your skills are evident — you are much more adept at laying out a body than I am. Besides, a partnership will give you a foothold in Pioche, saving you the expense of setting up your own shop."

We spent some time discussing the details. Marc encouraged me to order in chemicals for embalming, believing that sooner or later Pioche would settle down, with stable families and the accompanying desire for niceties such as ornate coffins, embalming, and elaborate funeral services.

And so I unpacked my embalming apparatus, oiled the belt, greased the pulleys, tightened the fittings, flushed the tubes and tested the pumping action. Six weeks later I fetched from the freight office two cases of Sphinx Embalming Fluid, shipped from the manufacturer in Syracuse, New York.

Marc's curiosity led to demonstrations of

the embalming equipment and numerous discussions about the processes involved. He seemed eager to see it done, so we were on the lookout for a likely candidate.

The opportunity came weeks later with the disappearance of a mining engineer who came to Pioche from the Mesabi Iron Range mines to ply his trade. As we were to learn, the young man struck out on his own after book-learning for the profession at the School of Mines at Columbia University, and apprenticeship in the Minnesota mines. His father, a wealthy mine owner and investor residing in Duluth, did not support the move, wanting for his son a more secure future in the family business.

I mentioned earlier the "disappearance" of the young engineer and it occurs the circumstances require explanation. Ownership of claims and mining properties around Pioche was a hopeless muddle. The complexities regarding outcrops and leads and lodes and lateral rights and the like kept legions of lawyers busy. More effective in the disputes — at least more decisive — were the gunmen hired to enforce one mine owner's notion of his rights over those of others with conflicting ideas.

The mining engineer in question seems to have been a victim of one such dispute. He left the mine of his employer late one evening to make his way home, but did not make it. Searchers gave up after a few days, finding no trace of the man nor any evidence of where he might have gone. His father left Dubuque for Pioche upon receipt of a wire from the mine owner, and while he was en route, a surveying crew found the engineer in a dry wash on the mountainside, well off the beaten path. A single bullet hole in the back of his head hinted at the reason for his demise.

Dicky and I carried the body out of the ravine on a litter to reach the road, loaded it in the handcart, and hauled it to the undertaking parlor. The engineer's father arrived the next day. He wished the body embalmed for transport back to Dubuque for burial in the family plot.

"At last," Marc said when the man left. "I'll get to see firsthand what this embalming's all about."

"We can do it," I said, "but I'm afraid the state of the body will not provide a typical example."

"How's that?"

"Decomposition. The corpse has been laying out there, exposed to the elements day after day. It doesn't look that bad, I know — likely owing to the dry climate — but on the inside I fear it's a whole different picture."

Still and all, we had a job to do and it would take us both to do it. I explained that under normal circumstances of arterial embalming, the pressure created by the centrifugal pump is sufficient to force the blood and fluids, the drainage, out of the arteries and veins and infuse the embalming chemicals in their place. With the mining engineer, however, the thickening of the blood and bodily fluids complicated things. The remedy is massage — and so it would be helpful to have Marc on hand to crank the pump slowly as I employed my hands and fingers to break up clots to allow the pressurized fluid to do its work.

And while a body with a single bullet wound in the head presented no difficulties under normal conditions, as the damage would not affect the circulatory system much, the decomposition of the engineer's body required multiple points of injection.

"It is not always so difficult, then," Marc said as we cleaned up afterward and clothed the body in a suit left for the purpose by his father.

"Oh, no. Nor so time consuming. This was about as bad a job as I've had. Hope to never have another like it."

Marc toweled off his hands after a good washing and suggested we replace some of our own lost fluid with a beer.

Like me, Marc was accustomed to drinking alone in the dim corners of saloons. Although more sociable than I, he found it difficult to strike up or maintain a conversation once folks learned he practiced The Dismal Trade. Unfair, I know — and as he and all undertakers know — but there it is. Most people will talk with undertakers only out of necessity.

We retired with our foamy mugs to a back table at Caucey's Saloon on the main street. The place was busy, with card players three deep around the green felt and four bartenders pouring drinks as fast as they could. A man with an accordion sat atop a tall stool in the corner across the way, his wheezing music box contributing to the confusion. I did not know any of the patrons, save two men at the next table. There sat the gunmen I had shared the stagecoach with in coming to Pioche. They looked us over when we came in: their faces revealing recognition but no awareness, and we were dismissed as offering no threat.

Lonigan, I remembered, was the quiet one's name. I did not know the name of the other, but had not forgotten his nasty, humorless laugh that from time to time overpowered the accordion and the general noise in the place.

The front door banged open, rattling the panes of glass in their rails and muntins. Silhouetted against the sunlight outside stood the mine owner from Dubuque. The thought crossed my mind that he may be looking for us, wondering about his son's body or to give us instructions for shipping.

Instead, he fixed his gaze on Lonigan's cohort.

Pulling a heavy revolver from a holster that looked out of place on him, he crossed the room and stopped before the gunfighters' table and pointed the pistol at the two, the barrel wavering back and forth between them.

Lonigan's chair screeched against the floor as he slid it back, his hand going to the butt of his pistol.

The laughing man did not move. He just smiled at the businessman. "What is it you want? What for are you comin' in here pointin' that gun at me? A man can get himself killed doin' that."

From where I sat, I could see him slowly slide his pistol from its sheath. In the din, you could not hear the ratcheting of the hammer as he pulled it back with his thumb.

The man from Dubuque shifted his attention from Lonigan. "You killed my son," he said through gritted teeth.

The gunman laughed his loud and obnoxious laugh. "Me? Your son? What the hell are you talkin' about?"

"Don't you dare deny it! I have made inquiries. While there is no direct evidence, there is little doubt it was you and your friend here who ambushed and executed him in a most cowardly fashion!"

Again, the braying laugh. "Made 'inquiries,' have you? Well, mister, I've got an 'inquiry' for you. What do you aim to do with that shootin' iron you're holdin' in your hand there?"

"I intend to take you two the marshal's office and swear out a complaint against you. For murder."

"Oh, you do, do you? What the hell for? Said yourself there's no evidence against us."

"Don't you worry. I'll find the evidence. Now, come along, both of you." He shifted his attention and the borehole of his gun barrel to Lonigan, who sat quietly through it all. "On your feet, now! Both of you!"

With another coarse laugh, the gunfighter put one hand atop the table and pushed himself to his feet. When the pistol in his other had cleared the edge of the table, he fired, the gun belching a cloud of white smoke.

The bullet that led the smoke out of the gun barrel struck the man from Dubuque dead center in the chest, the impact forcing him back two steps. His knees buckled and as he collapsed he pulled the trigger by reflex.

My forehead hit the table and the lights inside went out.

Chapter Thirteen

Before opening my eyes, I squinted them hard shut. It was, I suppose, a feeble attempt to pinch off the throbbing pain. Something cold and damp swiped across my forehead. I opened my eyes and waited for them to focus. When finally they did, I blinked and blinked again before realizing I was looking at the whitewashed ceiling of Caucey's Saloon, dulled by smoke and soot.

As if filtered through cotton, sound returned. The murmur of conversation. A breathy accordion.

I reached up to wipe away the tickle of something trickling down the side of my head, but the cold, wet rag I had felt earlier beat me to it.

"You all right, Pinebox?"

I winced as I turned toward the sound, and found Marc Henry's face looming. He again mopped my forehead with what must have been a bar rag. I looked the other way and there was the underside of a table.

Again, I squeezed my eyes tight shut. "What happened?"

"You got shot."

I flinched again as my eyes flew open, looking for something, somewhere, that would somehow make sense. "Shot?" The only thing that hurt was my head. "In the head?"

Marc laughed softly, and just as gently again wiped the trickle from my forehead. "No, son. You split your braincase when it hit the table. It's bleeding a good bit, but there ain't no real damage."

"Then where? Where was I shot?"

Again, the laugh. "The leg. You got shot in the leg."

With a grunt and groan I lifted myself on my elbows and studied my lower limbs, seeing no blood or bandages or anything else to mark a wound. I shook my head in confusion and lowered myself back to the floor.

"Same leg as before," Marc said with a laugh.

It hurt when I wrinkled my forehead.

"You remember the gunfight?"

"Yes. I think so. That mining engineer we embalmed — his father came in waving a pistol at those gunmen." But my memory went no further.

"Well, that feller from Duluth told them to get on their feet, as he was takin' them to the marshal's office. The loudmouthed one come up with gun in hand and shot him dead. The last thing that man did as he died was pull the trigger. Bullet hit that peg leg of yours — right about the dewclaws — and knocked it out from underneath you and upended you right where you sat. Your head smacked the edge of the table like a hammer hittin' an anvil."

"Help me up."

Marc wiped another trickle of blood from my forehead and tossed the rag onto the table. I reached out and grabbed his hands and he hefted me till I sat on my backside, then he grabbed me under the arms and pulled me to my feet, holding on till I steadied.

"I've got to sit down," I said as the room spun away.

With the toe of his shoe, Marc hooked a chair rail and dragged it over and turned and lowered me onto the seat. I swallowed hard, keeping the contents of my stomach in check. I looked around the room, and nothing seemed out of place.

"Where are they? The man from Minnesota, and the killer?"

"Long gone. The law came by and looked

things over. It was clear the dead feller started the whole affair, so the deputy told them gunslingers to clear out and stay out of trouble. Next time, he'd run them in, no matter. So they left. Dicky hauled the dead man over to the place. Laying there close to his son by now, I suspect. Reckon we'll be draining him, like we did his boy. Ship the two of 'em home together."

Everything Marc told me swirled around in my throbbing head as I stared vacantly around the room. "I must have been out for a while."

Again, Marc laughed, picked up the bloody towel, and sponged off my forehead. "That you were, son. Once everybody could see you'd likely survive the affray, they went on about their business like you wasn't even here."

I bent over — which elicited an involuntary moan — and grabbed my wooden leg, lifting it onto the opposite knee. The bullet had plowed a deep ditch along the side of the shank of the steer leg, starting in front just above the level of the dewclaws, tearing one off as it blew out the back. Chunks of the oak were missing, leaving jagged splinters, and the leg was split partway up along the grain. I grabbed the hoof and gave it a good shake and didn't cause any wobble or wiggle. Still, I would not trust the wood to hold up to the weight and wrenching of walking for any length of time. As much as I admired my steer leg, its days were done. The old original stump, packed away all these months in my trunk, would be recalled to duty until I manufactured a replacement.

"Hell of a thing to get shot twice in the same place," I said.

"That it is. The good Lord never took a likin' to that right leg of yours, for one reason or another."

Sucking in all the fetid saloon air my lungs could hold, I held my breath and tried to stand. Marc saw it coming and grabbed an elbow to help lift and steady me. The room settled into equilibrium after a moment, and I expelled the breath, drew another, and said, "Help me out the door if you will, Marc. I believe I should go home and sleep this off."

Home these days was a shabby boarding-house built to house miners, repaired after the big fire with a hodgepodge of salvaged lumber. Most of the rooms housed four beds and eight miners. The men occupied the beds in turn, sleeping either day or night depending on their shifts in the mines. For an added price — and a steep one at that — I had a room of my own.

"Room" overstates the situation considerably, however. Barely wide enough for a narrow bed jammed against two walls, there was just enough space for my trunk — still packed with my books and few other possessions not in daily service — against the foot of the bed. If I sat on the trunk, which I did every morning, I could slide my knees under a tiny washstand and wash up and shave courtesy of the hazy, cracked mirror hanging by a wire from a nail in the wall. Soap, shaving brush and mug, tooth powder and brush, and a comb filled a small drawer in the washstand, a drawer that required me to inhale in order to find room in the cramped quarters to slide open. My clothes hung on nails in the wall above the bed and sometimes awakened me in the night when the breeze through the wall brushed them against my face. All else — a few books, clothing waiting to be laundered, and odds and ends — lived on the floor under the bed, sharing the space with my peg leg when it reposed there at night.

While meals were included in my exorbitant rent, I seldom took more than one a day at the boardinghouse. Given the comings and goings of tenants at all hours, there were no regular mealtimes. Rather, the overburdened cook and her helper kept a sideboard in the eating room — I cannot call it a dining room — piled with whatever kinds of foods struck their fancy. Then men served themselves, heaping plates or bowls with gruel and stews and soups and sliced meats and boiled eggs and biscuits and bread and reconstituted desiccated vegetables and pickles and the like, all of varying ages and states of decomposition. Plates were scraped by their users into a slop bucket and dumped into a washtub. The soaking there may have been as close to washing as they got.

It was enough to make one pine for Hannah Morgan's rooming house in Kansas City.

But Pioche, Nevada, was a long way from Kansas City, in more ways than one. Here, laying out the dead and the occasional embalming took the place of the coffin building in Kansas City, which had taken the place of the undertaking work in Abilene and Springfield I was now back to. Marc and I were ever busy as the town kept growing, so undertaking was more in demand than woodworking.

Woodworking, however, was much on my mind. My old, original scratched and nicked-up wooden leg, handmade back in Nashville, served its purpose when once again called to duty. But its comfort left something to be desired, as did its plain and simple appearance. The steer leg had spoiled me, I suppose, and I wanted something more striking, so to speak.

And I had something in mind.

But wood was hard to come by in Pioche. Most of what the freighters hauled in went immediately down the mines as timber sets, cribbing, stulls, wedges, lagging, and the like. The rest went into buildings as fast as it could be pulled off the high-wheeled wagons, and was nailed up before the oxen were unyoked.

Few trees grew in that part of Nevada, and none suitable for lumber. Scant cottonwoods were the only variety of any size, their wood too soft to be of much use. Scrub oak flourished in the draws and ravines, but its girth was insufficient for anything much bigger than a toothpick. And so I turned to the numerous cedar trees — mountain juniper, according to the botany books — that stippled the ridges on most every mountainside. Seldom large enough to yield even a length of eight-by-eight square-set timber, the cedar trees did yield wood of beautiful variegated shades of color from cream to claret and, if harvested when dead and dried, plenty hard and strong enough to support a man with a wooden leg.

I spent a few afternoons riding or hobbling up and down the hills around Pioche in search of the perfect hunk of wood. A slash pile of dead cedar trees, cut to clear out construction around a mine shaft, offered up an ideal branch, out of which I sawed a suitable length.

I fetched my bag of woodworking tools out from under the workbench in the lean-to out back of the undertaking parlor. Since coming to Pioche, I'd had no need for any of the implements save a saw, plane, and hammer, with which I assembled coffins of simple design and serviceable quality when our usual supplier of wooden overcoats was backlogged. Embellishments of any kind weren't even discussed. After blowing off the dust and wiping off the oil, I lined up my chisels, gouges, skew, bent, veiner, knives, and mallet in a tidy row along the workbench.

Working only at odd hours when undertaking and daily life did not interfere, my new leg was weeks in the making. But after hand-rubbing the smoothed wood with varnish, lining the innards with padding, and screwing on the leather cuff and straps and belts, I found quiet satisfaction in its beauty.

Others, I soon learned, saw something else altogether in my new peg leg.

"That's a nasty lookin' thing you got strapped to your leg there," a night-shift miner said one morning between spoonfuls of boiled rolled oats sweetened with sorghum.

I hoisted my pant leg a few inches to give him the full effect. "I kind of like it, myself."

"Hmmph," he said, chomping a mouthful out of a thick ham sandwich. He studied the leg as I studied the sideboard for any trace of edible items, eventually deciding to take breakfast at a café I often frequented.

The serving girl — a rare youngster in Pioche, a child I judged to be no more than ten years old, daughter of the woman who owned and cooked at the eatery — tipped over my cup of coffee after bending over to fetch a dropped spoon, coming face to face with my workmanship, then bolting upright and grabbing at the table for support. My chair scraped the floor as I slid back to avoid the cascade dripping off the tabletop.

"I'm awful sorry, mister," the girl said, attempting to set down the spoon, put the cup upright, and mop up the spill with the skirt of her apron all at once.

"Are you all right?"

"Yessir," she said. "Sorry," still swiping at

145

the coffee, pushing the puddle around on the table more than soaking it up.

Her mother must have heard the racket from the kitchen. She came out with a mop rag and went to work on the spill.

"What's the matter, Miss Fumblefingers?"

"Took a fright, that's all, Ma."

The woman wadded the soaked rag and looked around. Only one other table was in use, its four occupants — shopkeepers and clerks waiting to go on duty — all looking on. "Don't see ary a thing in here to cause such a ruction."

Tugging at her mother's sleeve, the girl whispered something in the woman's ear.

"What?"

The girl repeated whatever it was.

The woman looked at the girl, looked at me, and back at the girl. "Land sakes, Ruthie, Mister Collins's been in here lots of times. His wood leg ought not scare you none. I know you've seed it before."

Again the girl pulled her down and whispered something more.

Again the mother shifted a curious glance from the girl to me, back, and again. She cleared her throat and stepped away from the table. "Mister Collins, let's have a look at that fake leg of your'n, if you don't care. I believe young Ruthie here is seein' things."

I obliged, turning in my seat, hiking up my pant leg as I lifted the appendage. The woman, eyes wide, took another step back. She bent over for a closer look, and stepped nearer.

"Lordy be, Mister Collins, that wood leg of yours looks for all the world like a snake."

Ruthie stepped beside her mother for an unobstructed view of the harmless likeness of a serpent. The men at the other table, overcome with curiosity, likewise wandered over for a look.

"Well I'll be damned," one said. "It sure enough looks like a rattlesnake, all right."

The other three only stared, along with the girl and woman. What they saw was, in fact, what looked to be a snake coiled around my shin, rattles and tail toward my knee and spade-shaped head extending out a bit where my foot used to be. A pattern of repeated diamond shapes were etched along the snake's back, reminiscent of, if not identical to, the markings of the diamond-back rattlers that frequented the area.

"What for'd'ya do that?" another of the store clerks said.

I smiled, maybe even laughed a little. "I needed a replacement when they shot my steer and crippled him."

It was no use to try and explain it to them

and relieve their bafflement. The fact is, I did not understand it myself.

CHAPTER FOURTEEN

As far off the beaten path as it was, Pioche was not altogether isolated. Brigham Young's Deseret Telegraph Company ran a line to Salt Lake City and Western Union's lines connected to San Francisco. Three newspapers served the city, my preferred rag being the *Lincoln County Leader.* Its coverage of local affairs was on a par with the other scandal sheets, but unlike its competitors, the *Leader* was not affiliated with either political party and attempted to stay neutral — meaning its editor was as likely to have everyone in a dither at one time or another, depending on the week's commentary.

But what attracted me to its pages was that it reprinted stories from newspapers across the country, some recent and received by wire, others gleaned from the columns of the printed papers that arrived in Pioche from time to time. One afternoon I came across an item reprinted from a Columbus or Cleveland or perhaps Cincinnati news-paper — I recall only that it was in Ohio — that was, by that time, several weeks past but still of enough interest that I clipped the article.

SCOUTS OF THE PLAINS
PLAIN "AWFUL"
— DO NOT TROUBLE YOURSELF
WITH THE PRODUCTION —

If you are inclined to take in a perfor-mance of "The Scouts of the Plains" dur-ing its engagement at the Orpheum The-atre, you would be well advised to save the two bits or invest it in a more reward-ing pastime — say a glass of weak and watered wine at one of our fair city's more mundane social clubs.

Handbills papering the town these past weeks promised "Daring Deeds! Elaborate Dresses! Full Dramatic Company!" Reality failed in every respect to live up to the hyperbole.

William F. "Buffalo Bill" Cody, "Texas Jack" Omohundro and "Wild Bill" Hickok are the titular Scouts of the show. While the first two of the trio delivered their lines with the derring-do one might expect of a western hero, their attempt at stentorian grandiloquence reeked of an amateur Shakespearean troupe.

Alas, "Wild Bill" proved much more cowardly in the recitation of his lines. Seemingly afraid of the footlights and the assembled audience, Hickok remained in the background, cowering behind scenery and props. Nonexistent memorization, and the long-haired Scout's weak and reedy voice, detracted from, rather than added to, the faltering affair.

The one dramatic moment Hickok did achieve was decidedly off-script, but entertaining nonetheless. About midway through the second act, "Wild Bill" was revealed in all his trembling timidity when the operator of a spotlight managed to capture him in the instrument's glow. Hickok shaded his eyes from the glare, shouted "Turn that d— n thing off!," drew his revolver, and shattered the arc light with a single well-placed shot.

I could not help but laugh aloud at the report. It must have been embarrassing for the fearless lawman of Abilene, the man I had watched face down a mob of Texas cowboys in Kansas City, to fail so at play-acting.

Pioche could have used a peace officer of

Hickok's abilities. While the local marshal and his deputies did their best to keep a lid on the town, the cemetery continued to host more than its share of occupants on "Murderer's Row." Some fell victim to gunfights in the street. More often, pistoleers in the employ of mine owners dry-gulched their opponents, shooting them down from ambush in hills around town. Seldom were the crimes solved, despite the efforts of the marshal's office.

The sheriff's office was something else altogether. Dealing more with serving warrants, collecting taxes, calling jurors, providing security in courtrooms, and running the jail than keeping the peace, the sheriff of Lincoln County carried more behind-the-scenes influence than the citizens who elected him were aware of. The office was much sought after, mostly for the purported $40,000 in bribes and graft that came with the badge in an average year.

Bob Logan had a firm grip on the office during most of my time in Pioche. Rumor had it he paid voters well for their support. Business owners routinely forked over the additional "taxes" he assessed rather than risk the difficulties he could cause, including revoking their business and commercial licenses for invented infractions.

He was, I suppose, adequate for the job, but like many a lawman he let the power go to his head. Logan came to Pioche from California, where they say he had a wife and family. In Pioche, he kept a room at the Palace Hotel but seldom, word had it, rumpled the sheets there. Persistent rumors said his preferred abode was at a house of ill repute run by Maria Quintana, where he shared the room — and bed — of the proprietor when she was not entertaining guests on those occasions when demand outstripped the supply of available girls. Hers was a high-class establishment, catering to mine officers, city officials, lawyers, business managers, and the like, rather than working men. As far as I was concerned, it was all just gossip, most likely spread by Logan's political rivals.

A knock on my door sometime in the hours after midnight but before dawn led to my one and only encounter with Bob Logan.

The pounding bolted me upright and out of the bed. I stumbled, lurched across the slender space between the cot and the wall, bumping my head and scuffing the knee on my good leg. Fortunately, hitting the wall prevented my falling to the floor. I sat back onto the bed as the banging started up again. This time, I stood and balanced a hand against the wall, hopped to the door, and opened it. There stood Dicky, fist raised to pummel the door again.

I rubbed my face with the palm of my hand and raked back my hair with my fingers. "What is it, Dicky?"

"Mister Henry, he says for you to come. There's two dead. He wants you."

Massaging the corners of my eyelids with thumb and forefinger to wipe the sleep away, I asked where.

"Miss Quintana's whorehouse, that's where."

"What happened?"

"Shot. Two bodies. C'mon."

I yawned and shook my head like a dog shedding water. "You go on ahead. I'll be along."

"Mister Henry, he says for me to wait."

I yawned again. "All right. Give me a minute."

Dicky stood propping the door open and watched wide-eyed as I sat on the bed to button my shirt and pull on my pants and shoe.

"You reading that?" he said with a nod toward the book sitting atop my trunk.

"I am."

"What's it about?"

Again, I scrubbed my face with my hands before reaching under the bed to pull out my peg leg. "It's called The *Ingenious Nobleman Sir Quixote of La Mancha,* but it mostly just goes by *Don Quixote.* He wanders around Spain trying to right wrongs and do good deeds. Mostly, though, he doesn't have much of a grasp on what's going on," I said as Dicky watched me strap on the snake.

"Don't read much, me. Letters gets all jumbled and I can't keep track. Wouldn't bother with a book that fat."

Hands on the edge of the bed, I pushed myself upright. "Let's get going."

Keeping up with Dicky was a job for a man with two good legs. Stumping along on one and a hunk of wood was too much to ask. He would stop from time to time and stand with his hands in his pockets, studying the ground as he scuffed it around with his feet. About the time I'd catch up, he'd turn on a heel and stride off again.

Huffing and hobbling, I made it to Quintana's brothel to see a body in the dooryard and another draped down the front porch steps. Another man sat on the street in front of the narrow yard, hands overhead and cuffed to the hitching rail. In the dim light falling out the open front door, I could see the town marshal talking with Miss Quintana on the porch, she dressed in a sheer nightgown with a shawl over her shoulders to conceal what her sleeping attire did nothing to hide. Something must be up, I thought, to get the marshal out of bed. Now and then I got a glimpse of the working girls as they came and went behind their madam; others leaned out open windows upstairs.

Marc and a deputy stood to one side, our handcart creating a barrier between the bodies and a small group of onlookers. I joined the two men and asked about the bodies.

"Remember those two gunmen in Caucey's place the night you got shot? That's the loudmouthed one cuffed to the hitching rail there. His pal — the one that never talked much, if ever — is the dead one in the yard."

"Lonigan's his name," I said. "Don't know the name of the other one. For all the talking he does, I never heard him say his name."

"Name's Drury," the deputy said. "Garland Drury. I've had more than a few run-ins with them two. They're smart enough that nothin' sticks, though. Always manage to goad a man into pulling a gun on 'em so's it's self-defense. We're right sure they're dry-gulchin' cowards, too, but we can't get no evidence on 'em. 'Security guards' they call 'em up at the Consolidated. But they ain't nothin' more'n the same kind of hired killers that work for the rest of the mines."

"Who's that on the steps?"

Marc's mouth twitched with a hint of a smile. "Bob Logan."

"The sheriff?"

"The same."

I looked again. "He's in his nightshirt!"

The deputy said, "That he is. Don't know if you know it, but he spends most nights cuddled up with Miss Quintana."

I'd heard the rumors but hadn't really believed them. Reports of his activities in the *Lincoln County Leader* often mentioned that our elected sheriff was a man of honor. Reported to be husband and father to a fine family still residing back home in Tulare, California, where they would stay until he felt it safe enough to bring them to Pioche and he could once again reside in the bosom of his loved ones. As I said, I'd heard rumors otherwise, but had no reason to believe them until now.

I pondered the situation for a few minutes. "What happened?"

A loud laugh turned our attention to the man I now knew as Drury, standing, but still hitched to the rail. The marshal stood across the rail from him, arms akimbo and

157

leaning into the gunman's face, saying something we could not hear, through gritted teeth.

"He's laughin' now, just like always," the deputy said. "We'll see how funny he thinks it is when whoever takes over as sheriff strings a noose around his neck. We got him dead to rights this time."

I repeated my question.

Marc cleared his throat. "Seems the two gunmen came calling, looking for a lawyer — whose name I will not mention — they'd been told was visiting at Miss Quintana's. Pounded on the door raising all kinds of fuss. When they wouldn't go away at Maria's invitation, the sheriff came out wearing nothing but his nightshirt and gun belt to see what they wanted.

"They said their boss at the mine wanted them to 'interview' the attorney about a lawsuit he'd filed against the Consolidated. Logan told them to get the hell out of there and make an appointment at the lawyer's office during business hours, like civilized folks. From what Miss Quintana said, things got nasty and Bob drew his gun and shot Lonigan. Drury shot him at the same instant. Three shots fired — one by the sheriff, and two into his chest from Drury's gun. Girls said it sounded like only two shots, the first ones came so close together. Once the smoke cleared, they saw what you're seeing now."

"Well, deputy, sounds like Drury has a good claim for self-defense."

Again, Drury's horse laugh sounded from over at the hitch rail. The deputy's laugh was much softer.

"I'm bettin' he thinks so, and that's why he's takin' on. Thing is, that whore of Logan's says she'll swear Drury shot Bob first, but he finished drawin' his gun and shot Lonigan 'fore he fell. Then Drury shot the sheriff ag'in, and that time he fell dead. The rest of the whores'll back her up."

The marshal hailed the deputy over, and he held a gun on Garland Drury as the marshal unlocked the cuff from one of the gunman's wrists and reattached it with both hands behind the prisoner's back. The deputy waved us a goodbye as he shoved Drury into motion and started off toward the jail. The marshal told us we might as well get the bodies out of there before morning. Dicky wheeled the cart over and he and I hefted Lonigan in and pushed him aside as Marc and the marshal hauled the sheriff's body down the steps and to the cart.

Marc and I watched as Dicky rolled away.

The sky to the east was showing silver as Marc said, "I reckon we might as well drain the sheriff and pump him full with those chemicals of yours and box him up for shipping. Unless I miss my bet, his wife and family will want him back in California."

Lonigan, on the other hand, would likely end up in a shallow grave on Murderer's Row in the Pioche cemetery. I doubted that even Garland Drury would bother to mourn his passing.

Drury was tried, but not convicted, for the murder of the night-shirted sheriff. He claimed self-defense, as expected. Quintana and her working girls testified otherwise, but the jury refused to believe stories told by common whores — their refusal encouraged, some said, by covert cash payments from the Consolidated Mining Company.

CHAPTER FIFTEEN

Sheriff Bob Logan's remains rode out of town atop a stagecoach bound for Palisades and a connection on the transcontinental rails to California. Logan would, most likely, arrive at his destination undisturbed even if the coach was robbed. Even the greediest road agents were loath to open a coffin.

But there was little else the outlaws wouldn't do.

For quite some time, a spate of robberies had kept local law enforcement officers and agents hired by the stage line riding hard up and down desert mountains and across sage-covered plains in pursuit of a bandit who bested them at every turn. Sometimes he held up coaches on his own, pilfering the Wells Fargo express box and relieving passengers of anything that looked valuable. Other times it was crew of masked bandits, complete with pack animals, who hauled off the Wells Fargo box intact — often when it contained a payroll for one of the mines — along with other express freight packages from the coach.

Drivers and law officers, and some of the passengers who witnessed holdups, swore Jack Harris was behind the robberies. But there was no evidence to be had, and no matter what schemes they cooked up to entrap him, Harris always managed to give the law the slip.

Tired of the losses, the manager of the express office in Pioche decided it would be cheaper to pay Harris a handsome wage as a "security consultant" to meet incoming coaches and oversee the unloading of the Wells Fargo box. He took the job.

The banditry continued without interruption.

Oh, Harris was there at the stage station to meet every arrival, earning his pay. He'd show up a few minutes ahead of the coach and stand on the porch puffing away on a fat cigar. A good-natured sort of fellow, Harris laughed and joked with the drivers and shotgun guards, and commiserated with them when they reported yet another robbery.

Only once did I cross paths with Harris; one time when expecting rush delivery of a carton of embalming chemicals. I was awaiting the arrival of the stage late one afternoon. Harris showed up shortly after I did. He seemed out of breath, but I attributed it to his hotfooting it from an alley down the street a ways. A cigar came out of his pocket and he went through the ritual of lighting it, after which he offered me one of the smokes.

"Meaning no disrespect, I'll decline your offer," I said. "I don't partake of tobacco — it disagrees with me."

"As you wish. No offense taken." He tucked the offered stogie back into his pocket, expelled a cloud of rank smoke, and asked about my peg leg.

For what must have been the hundredth time, I launched into the tale but hadn't got far when we heard a bugle blast from the driver, soon followed by the jingle of trace chains and the snorting and blowing of teams as the stagecoach pulled up. The whip and the guard were in a foul mood, reporting another holdup.

"Wasn't more'n five miles out," the guard said. "Sonofabitch piled a heap of brush and rocks in the road comin' out of a turn. Barely got the teams hauled in, or it would've upended the whole shebang. Then he stepped out from behind a cedar tree. Had the drop on us 'fore we even knew what was happenin'.""

As the shotgun rider mumbled obscenities under his breath and the office agent stewed, Harris, thumbs in the armholes of his vest, rocked back on his heels and smiled around his smoking cigar. "What'd he get?"

"Shot the locks off the Wells Fargo box and relieved it of some pouches," the guard said. "Took what he could get from them on board. Few other things."

"What about my shipment?" I said.

The guard and driver scowled and both asked what it was.

I used my hands to show the dimensions of the small crate. "Just a wooden box about so. Would have been labeled 'glass' or 'fragile' or 'handle with care' or something like that."

"Oh, yeah," the driver said. "The bastard took that, too. Said he thought it might be some wine or whiskey or somethin' too fancy to be in a reg'lar shipment."

The confusion surrounding the robbery and loss reports by the passengers continued as hostlers led away the teams and hitched up fresh horses. Harris stood by sucking his cigar. He blew out a stream of smoke, waved the smoldering stogie in my direction.

"What was in that box of yours?"

"Embalming fluid."

"What?"

"Embalming fluid. I'm an undertaker. Partners with Marc Henry. We had a run of folks to lay out on account of an accident out in Bullionville. Couldn't wait for regular delivery, or even fast freight, so I had a few bottles shipped in express."

Harris took a long draw on his cigar and expelled another cloud of smoke. "Check back tomorrow. Could be it got mixed up somewheres."

The express agent must have overheard our talk. "Ain't likely," he said. "Harris, you know our people are right careful about that sort of thing. Don't get the man's hopes up. That outlaw took it, it's probably already been dumped in the desert somewhere."

"You come along anyway, undertaker," Harris said as he tossed the butt of his cigar into the street, causing one of the hitched horses to shy and a hostler to grab the headstall and calm it down. "Could be you'll get lucky."

I stopped by the stage line office the next day on Harris's say-so. Lo and behold, there was the box. It had obviously been pried open and lid nailed back on, but the six bottles in their lining of excelsior were unbroken.

Harris's kindness — or whatever you

165

choose to call it — proved the man's undo-ing.

Suspicious of how Harris could have known anything about my package, and surprised when it turned up as predicted, the express office agent gave him his next assignment and then put a tail on him. The next time I heard about Harris was a report in the *Leader* concerning his arrest and confession. You can't trust everything you read in the newspaper, but the talk around town supported the basics of the story.

As suspected, Harris was behind at least most of the holdups. He had numerous hideouts in the desert and mountains, including some in abandoned mines. A network of trails and shortcuts allowed him to move about at will following robberies, with pursuers following decoy paths, taking wrong turns, and losing the track for other reasons.

When hired by the express company, he held up the stage and then beat it back to Pioche on back trails and cutoffs, arriving in plenty of time to take up his post on the stage station porch to greet the arriving coach and hear, firsthand, reports of his own exploits.

As for me, I cannot help but think kindly of Jack Harris. He could have easily used my bottles of embalming chemicals for target practice, poured the fluid into the dust, or simply abandoned them under the cedar tree where he stashed them, rather than see to their return.

Should he hang for his crimes, I will be pleased to lay him out and see he gets a proper burial at my own expense.

Not so with another Pioche ne'er-do-well. But I will have to back up a bit to tell the story of Jim Levy.

Levy was a hired gun in the shape of Lonigan and Drury, working for one of the mining companies as an enforcer. Given that intimidation and shooting did not occupy all their time, most of these gunslingers spent more time than is healthy hanging around Pioche's saloons drinking whiskey and telling lies and bragging about their abilities as gunfighters — those last two activities being one and the same, if you ask me. If all those gun hands had left as many bodies behind as they claimed, my chosen profession would require a lot more practitioners than there are people who answered the latest government census.

But Levy's story starts with just such a bragging contest in the Overland Saloon. Hired guns Tom Gossan and Mike Casey carried on a dispute for days, weeks even, each claiming to be the superior gunfighter. The quarrel spilled onto the street one afternoon, with the two facing off with deadly intent. Casey got the best of Gossan, his bullets finding their mark. Bleeding and dying but not giving up the fight, Gossan's last wish was for someone — anyone — of his friends to kill Mike Casey. And he told of $5,000 cash in an envelope concealed under a drawer in his hotel room, bequeathed to the successful assailant of his mortal enemy.

Well, Jim Levy learned of the offer and intended to collect. He spent a long night drinking in the Overland Saloon. Fortified by liquid courage, Levy trumpeted his intention to kill Casey at first opportunity. That opportunity wasn't long in coming.

"Mike Casey just went into Freudenthal's store!" a street loafer hollered upon entering the Overland Saloon, but his announcement was mostly intended for Levy's ears. Levy nursed his drink and paid little attention. Saloon patrons, having listened to Levy's long and loud threats, prodded him to go after his quarry but Levy did nothing. The crowd's encouragement turned to insults, questioning the gunman's courage. The jeering stopped when Levy stood and drew his gun and fired a shot into the ceiling, his bullet knocking glass danglers from the Overland's ostentatious chandelier, causing the fixture to tinkle and chime in the otherwise silent, smoky room.

"I'll shoot the first sonofabitch that calls me a coward," Levy said, unsteady on his feet. His eyes followed the barrel of his pistol back and forth across the room. Hearing no further affronts, he holstered the pistol and sat back down.

"Meanin' no disrespect, Jim," a man standing at the bar said, "you said you'd kill Casey first chance you got."

"So?"

"Well, here's your chance."

Levy grimaced and threw back the last of the whiskey in his glass. He stood, reset the hat on his head, checked the loads in his revolver and replaced the spent cartridge. Pushing through the saloon door, he stopped on the sidewalk, drew in a long breath of the morning air, adjusted his gun belt, and stepped off the boardwalk into the street.

I'd just come out of a greasy spoon café and was putting a toothpick to work when I saw Levy stop in the middle of the street. His stance wasn't as steady as you'd expect of a man intending gunplay, so I did not know at the time what he was up to. He

169

fingered the grip on his pistol for long seconds while I wondered.

The door to Freudenthal's opened and Mike Casey stepped out, his fingers stroking the brim edge of a new Stetson hat of the "Boss of the Plains" style popular among Western types.

"Mike Casey!" Levy shouted.

The shout startled Casey. No sooner had the shopper identified the source of the call than smoke gushed from Levy's pistol and the bullet it followed punched a red hole in Casey's stomach some three inches above and slightly to the right of the buckle on his idle gun belt.

Casey's right hand covered the wound, and he looked in disbelief at the blood that escaped his grasp, leaking out between his fingers. He took two hesitant steps and sat down, propped up by a porch post.

Levy, smoke still wisping from his gun, walked slowly toward Casey. People watching expected another shot, but Levy did not pull the trigger. Upon reaching the dying man, he raised the revolver and swung it at full strength, the barrel breaking a bloody gash in Casey's head. He repeated the blow three, four, five times until the dead man tipped over and rolled off the sidewalk and fell onto the dusty street.

Wiping the bloody barrel of his pistol on Casey's shirt, he looked the gun over and dropped it into its holster. He looked around at the growing crowd as if expecting to hear something, but the only response was stunned silence. Levy smiled and belched. "Five thousand dollars," he said. "Not bad for a morning's work."

He started off down the street but stopped when he drew even with me. "Well, don't just stand there, you peg-legged sonofabitch. Get that trash cleaned up off the street."

CHAPTER SIXTEEN

Lacking family or anyone at all who cared, Mike Casey's mortal remains went into a grave on Murderer's Row, housed in a rough coffin and without benefit of embalming. Few people in Pioche paid his passing any note. One who did was Garland Drury. Having lost his pal Lonigan in the gunfight with Sheriff Bob Logan, he'd taken up with Casey, the two of them forming something of a friendship, most likely spurred by a lack of alternatives.

Drury's bellicose behavior and loud, irritating laughter was off-putting to most. My acquaintance with Casey being limited to conveying him into the afterlife, I cannot comment on why so few people sought his friendship. Mirroring Levy's behavior when announcing his intention to kill Casey, Drury let it be known loud and long that he had Jim Levy in his sights for killing his friend.

Meanwhile, Levy, fearing it was only a matter of time before the law tracked him down and tried him for what the court would surely see as Casey's cold-blooded murder, collected his $5,000 reward, packed his bag, and bought a ticket on the next stage out of Pioche. The stagecoach was at the station, fresh teams hitched and ready to load passengers, when Drury showed up, gun in hand.

"Levy! Where are you? You cowardly son-ofabitch!"

Stepping out from behind the coach, where he'd been watching the shotgun guard stow his money-stuffed carpet bag in the boot, Levy pulled his pistol before answering. Aiming the revolver at Drury, he said, "Take a look, loudmouth. I'll be the last thing you see."

Drury dropped to a knee as he turned. Levy wasn't fooled, and pulled the trigger before Drury got his gun around. The bullet drilled a scorched hole near the center of Drury's forehead and he fell nose-first into the street, his face landing in a steaming pile of dung left by one of the coach horses.

It would be a pleasure, I thought, to be the undertaker to clean that off his cold, dead features.

Not wanting to wait around for the stage after shooting Drury, Levy grabbed his bag from the boot and with long strides crossed the street toward a man who sat horseback, watching the ruckus.

"Get off the horse!"

"What?" the rider said.

"Get off!"

"Like hell I will."

Levy lifted the revolver still in his hand and ratcheted back the hammer as its bore-hole stared at the man. The rider swung out of the saddle and held the rein out to Levy.

"Take this," Levy said, shoving the carpet-bag into the man's chest. "Tie it behind the saddle."

The man dropped the rein and did so. Shoving the horse's owner aside, the gun-fighter stepped into the stirrup and found a seat in the saddle, jerked the horse around, and, pounding its flanks with his boot heels, galloped down the main street and out of Pioche into the desert beyond.

By the time I fetched Dicky and the cart, the clouds that had been streaming across the sky all morning were piled up in roiling black waves. The wind whipped up as we rolled the cart up the hill and by the time I had Drury laid out on the slab and started undressing him, raindrops pounded the roof. Marc brought a bundle of mail in from the front office and offered to finish the job if I would take the letters to the post office and run a few other errands in town. Having had my fill of Garland Drury while he was alive, I welcomed the respite from his presence in death.

The rain fell by the bucket as I made my way through the streets, and before covering two blocks I was saturated and dripping water droplets like a raincloud. My shoe and peg leg seemed to sink deeper with every step into the mud, and its slimy buildup weighed me down and made footing uncertain. And so I decided to detour to the boardinghouse to wait out the storm, or at least take shelter until the worst of it passed.

The drumming on the roof continued as I reclined on my cot, clothed only in dry underwear but wrapped in a blanket, absorbed by the exploits of Lady Dedlock, John Jarndyce, Esther Summerson, and the rest of the people Charles Dickens brought to life in the pages of *Bleak House*. So engrossed was I that I barely noticed when the rain slackened then stopped some three hours later, perhaps fooled by the continued dripping from roof ledges and the streaming rivulets in the streets.

When I finally set the book aside, donned

dry clothes, turned up the collar of my coat, and stumped my way to the street, I could scarcely believe what the storm had dumped on Pioche. The flood streams I had heard fed down to other streets, gathering strength until becoming a river. The floodwaters, thick with mud and clogged with debris, tore through the lower streets of the city, knocking houses off their footings, crashing through walls, undermining foundations, and carrying entire buildings away.

Navigating the streets proved nearly impossible, what with all the trash and newly eroded ditches and washouts in the streets. I hurried as fast as my peg leg could carry me, slipping and sliding and sinking my way down the hill to see what had become of the undertaking parlor.

What I found was a jumbled pile of logs. It looked like a wall of water and rubble hit the side of the building, collapsing the wall, which caused the roof to cave in, taking with it the other walls. Then, the whole mess shifted downhill several feet, churning as it went.

Dicky was already there, staring helplessly at the handcart, which had lost a wheel, the other hanging from a shattered axle, both shafts and the crossbar broken off and missing.

"Dicky! Help me! I think Marc is in here!"

Dicky sauntered over, hands in pockets, eyes glazed over.

"Help!"

Appearing unaware of what he was doing, he grabbed the other end of a log and together we shifted it, wrenched it free and heaved it aside. Dicky caught on to what needed to be done and we pawed into the wrecked building, tossing away cedar limbs, mud-soaked sagebrush, tangled wads of rabbit brush, broken boards, discarded pieces of used mine timber, poles from the roof, furniture and fixtures from the parlor, and we strained and struggled with logs from the fallen walls.

Other men came to help; some in soiled business suits, others in rough miners' clothing. More came as the mines hoisted men out of the shafts, forsaking the ore to help with the emergency in the town. Two mineworkers helped me dislodge a smashed tabletop from the wreckage, revealing a mud-covered body beneath.

A miner said, "That your man?"

"No," I said through labored gasps. "He's naked. Must be Garland Drury. Had him laid out."

I straddled the face-down body, grasping it under the arms. I heaved Drury out of the thick, slimy mud, raising him half a foot, maybe a foot, but no more before the cold, slimy corpse slipped from my hands to fall back into the slop.

"Lemme at 'im," a miner said. He reached into the mud and came up with a wrist, and signaled his coworker to do the same. I winced when Drury's elbows and shoulders popped and cracked as they wrenched him loose.

"Don't you worry none, laddie. He ain't feelin' it." I heard one of the miners say.

They dragged Drury away and I could see the legs and feet of Marc Henry. Marc must have been standing beside the table working on the body when the flood hit, tipping the table over, knocking Marc off his feet, and dumping Drury atop him.

Accustomed as I was to being in the presence of death, I nevertheless scrambled out of the mess and collapsed onto a seat on a wet, mud-covered log. Then I stuck my head between my knees and vomited again and again into the debris until I could heave no more. The men stopped working and looked on. Several wandered away, the purpose behind the work fulfilled. A few stayed on to help the two miners who'd found the bodies clear away enough of the tangled mess to free Marc. I was grateful they went about it more gently than they had with Drury.

Dicky drifted about aimlessly, still somewhat unhinged by the whole situation. He came over to me and tried without success to brush the mud off the log beside me, gave it up, and sat down. We sat in silence for a few minutes, then I felt Dicky's arm around my shoulders. He gave me a squeeze, left his arm there, and just sat.

Marc Henry was the last body I prepared for burial in Pioche, and one of the few not planted in Murderer's Row. Like Drury, he went into the ground unembalmed. It took a few days combing through the flotsam to salvage any usable equipment. I found the centrifugal pump used for embalming, but it was so permeated with mud it could not be put back in working order soon enough to do Marc any good. Besides which, the bottles of embalming chemicals were broken and the tubes and needles gone.

While not as dramatic, perhaps, as the rain of frogs I had witnessed in Kansas City, the consequences of the storm and flood in Pioche were much more consequential. Nearly three and a half inches of rain fell in two hours, give or take. This, in a high desert where a good year brings maybe a foot of rain. Marc Henry's undertaking establishment was one of twenty-two buildings destroyed by the flash flood, with dozens more damaged.

Day after day, Dicky and I sifted through the debris, digging out anything useful. I salvaged most of my woodworking tools, some already showing rust under the mud that coated them. I scoured them clean, coated them with a light sheen of oil, and stowed them in a war surplus duffel bag from Freudenthal's store. The case for the embalming pump also turned up, albeit in a pile of refuse some ways down the hill, with all the gadgets and fittings in their proper places. I washed the mud off it and packed the scrubbed-up pump inside. When I fixed shut the latches, I wondered when — or if — I would ever again open that case.

Scavengers worked the ruined buildings of the town, looking for salvageable lumber. Probably owing to the fact that our wreckage formerly housed an undertaking establishment, few came nosing around our wall logs. Lacking the stomach to rebuild, I allowed anyone who asked to tote the logs and any useable lumber away. Anything left went up in a bonfire.

Marc having no known family heirs, and me being his partner, both the business and the property came to me. As I said, I had no wish to rebuild, or even continue in Pioche. I sold the town lot on which the building used to stand before the flash flood it could not withstand knocked it down. Half the money from the sale I gave to Dicky. The rest, save pocket money, went into the trunk along with my books and clothes and spare leg.

And so I said farewell to the town of Pioche on its tenuous mountainside perch and boarded a northbound stagecoach for Palisades. There, I would purchase a train ticket on the transcontinental railroad. What direction that train would take, where I would get off, or what I would do when I did, I did not know.

CHAPTER SEVENTEEN

A train whistle sounded in the distance, spurring the people of Palisades to action. Would-be robbers entered the bank. Faux lawmen pinned on badges and checked the loads in their revolvers to reassure themselves the cartridges were blanks. Women and children took their places in the street and on the boardwalks, waiting for panic to ensue.

Gunfire echoed off the bluffs from which the town took its name as the train rolled slowly into the station, drawing the attention of the passengers. The outlaws shot their way out of the bank and mounted skittish horses, firing all the while at the townsmen and law officers who returned fire from behind water troughs, the corners of buildings, even from second-story windows of the tallest structure in town. Women tugged children's hands, hurrying them to safety. Even the town's dogs got in on the action, barking and nipping at the hooves of the horses.

I stepped onto the train and found a seat in time to see the bandits — those of them not lying in the street — ride out of town at a high lope, turning in the saddle to get off a few more shots as the men in their good-guy roles for this performance stood in the street firing at the retreating robbers.

All was once again quiet and peaceful in Palisades before the town was out of sight. I did not interrupt the excited discussions among the passengers to explain it was all play-acting. Nevada's landscape along the rail line offers few other distractions, and so I let them relive the excitement and remain unaware of its falsity.

As it happened, the first train out of Palisades after my arrival was eastbound, so that was the train I was on. I purchased a ticket that would take me to the next city of any note, that being Ogden, in Utah Territory, where I would transfer to the Utah Central Railroad for a short ride south to Salt Lake City. Why, I did not know. But being at loose ends, it seemed as good an idea as any.

The rails followed the Humboldt River across much of Nevada, the route followed by 49ers racing for gold as well as most of the California-bound settlers since. We passed into Utah and the white glare of the salt desert and saw little else but sagebrush until reaching the Wasatch Mountains. The trip provided ample time to read from Nathaniel Hawthorne's romantic novel, *The Scarlet Letter.* I would soon learn the puritanical views and hypocrisy about which Hawthorne wrote were still practiced in the Mormon kingdom into which the rails carried me.

Unlike the hodgepodge and chaos of Pioche, Salt Lake City proved the most orderly, tidy, enterprising metropolis of my experience. Wide streets followed compass points, dividing the city into large blocks. In residential areas, houses lined the streets, with vegetable gardens watered from roadside ditches, and barns, livestock pens, and outbuildings in the backlots.

The business district bustled, if quietly. People went about their work with determination, passing in and out of the buildings, dodging drays and carriages and horse-drawn vehicles of every description in the streets. The centerpiece of the city was the looming gray walls of a house of worship, a temple, rising out of the ground. To its west stood the "tabernacle," looking for all the world like a giant shingled turtle.

I took a room at the Farnham Hotel until more permanent lodging arrangements could be located. The manager, Elijah Abel, was a black man, and one of the few colored faces to be found in the city. I spent days walking the streets of the business district and nearby neighborhoods, seeing a handful of undertaking establishments in my travels. I did not inquire about employment, still unsure if I wanted to return to The Dismal Trade following the unfortunate end to my experience in Pioche. On the other hand, I assumed the work here would involve fewer victims of gunfights or other violence, considering Salt Lake City seemed to be a more peaceful place.

That was before I met Porter Rockwell. But I will get to that.

One day as I strolled down a quiet street on the verge of the residential area, I passed a small commercial building displaying a "Help Wanted" sign in the window. The only other sign or identification of any kind was painted on the window above: ALONZO HADLEY, CABINETRY & JOINERY.

I tried the door and found it unlocked and stepped into a large room crowded with cabinets and furniture in various states of completion. Although crowded, the room was in no way cluttered — everything appeared to be methodically arranged and well-ordered. Along the side and rear walls were workbenches, tools, and machinery; the floor carpeted with sawdust and shavings. A soft tap-tap-tap came from somewhere.

"Mister Hadley?"

The tapping stopped. "Yes?" The man stepped out from behind a tall wardrobe or highboy. A face framed by wiry graying hair and beard made his age hard to determine. He set a mallet atop an unfinished chest of drawers, rubbed his hands on his apron front, and extended a handshake.

"Alonzo Hadley," he said. "And who might you be, young man?" I handed him a card, which he studied for a moment, then laughed. "An undertaker, are you, Jonathon 'Pinebox' Collins? I am getting up there in years, but am not of the opinion that I will be needing your services anytime soon."

I felt my face redden. "Oh, no, sir! I beg your pardon. I only meant it to give my name. I came about the sign in the window."

Hadley pursed his lips and thought for a moment, then said. "I am a cabinetmaker and joiner, Mister Collins. My work is with wood — sawing, planing, joining, molding, gluing, veneering, carving, finishing — that type of thing, don't you see."

"Yes, Mister Hadley. I know. I am sorry for the confusion. Besides undertaking, I have built many a coffin. Most plain, for certain, and nothing of the quality of your craftsmanship. I have also done some finish carpentry, and learned a bit about furniture making from my father. So I am familiar with the tools of your trade and know the basics of woodworking — enough so, I believe, that I could be of service to you."

Hadley thought it over, again with pursed lips, then invited me to follow him. He sat on a tall stool at a workbench and gestured toward a spindle-back chair. I took a seat, not bothering to sweep off the film of sawdust.

"Where is it you've built these coffins of yours, Mister Collins?"

"Please — call me Jon. Pinebox if you'd rather. Jonathon, even." I cleared my throat. "Kansas City, for the most part. I had a small shop there, supplying many of the city's undertakers. Before that, in Abilene. Lately in Pioche, although in those places I mostly did undertaking and embalming, making coffins for my own use — well, for use by my clients."

We talked some more about my know-how with wood. I hoisted my pants cuff and extended my coiled-snake peg leg. He looked it over, and asked how I came to lose my leg. With that story told, he opined that the workmanship showed some skill.

Then, he said, "Would you be willing to rough out the work, maybe do some gluing and sanding, apply oil and varnish and the like? Leave the finer work to me?"

"Of course."

"As time passes, I may teach you some of the finer points of the trade. But as for the future, you need to know right now that I have two sons. Younger than you, but not much. Both boys worked with me and will do so again, once they return from their missionary work for the church. The business will be theirs. I do not want to lead you to believe there will be a long-term future here, as that may not — likely will not — be the case. Are you willing to go to work on those terms?"

"Yes, Mister Hadley. That will suit me fine."

"Good. No more of this 'Mister Hadley' then. As is our custom here, please call me 'Brother' if you don't mind. I will do the same. You will be Brother Collins inside these walls."

It would be awkward, it seemed, to call a man old enough to be my father "Brother," but I determined to try the formality. We talked pay and expectations and such and shook hands to confirm the agreement just as the front door opened. Whoever it was did not wait, as footsteps padded across the floor without hesitation.

"Ah, Emma," Hadley said to the woman. "It must be time for dinner."

She looked to be well into middle age, wore an apron over her housedress, and a bonnet on her head. In her hands was a woven basket, a checked cloth covering whatever it held.

"Emma, this is Brother Collins. He is not of our faith, but is our brother all the same. Brother Collins will be helping me in the shop. Brother Collins, this is my wife Emma."

The woman bowed slightly, but neither spoke nor smiled.

"I am pleased to meet you, Emm— Sister Em— Sister Hadley."

Brother Hadley said, "Will you join me for a bite, Brother Collins?"

The suggestion seemed to trouble Sister Hadley, so I refused as politely as possible, claiming a need to be elsewhere. Not altogether true, but not exactly a lie, either. The woman looked relieved. I told my new employer I would see him come morning ready to go to work, and took my leave. In order to stay honest, I decided to spend the afternoon looking for a place to stay.

Back at the Fordham, I unstrapped my leg and stretched out on the bed with copies of yesterday's *Deseret Evening News* and this morning's *Salt Lake Tribune,* combing the classified advertisements for a place offering room and board. While the classified listings were similar, elsewhere the newspapers could not have been more different.

The *Tribune* had nothing good to say about the Mormon church, its leaders, its practices, or its dominance over the Territory and its people, Mormons and the few "Gentiles" alike. The *Deseret Evening News* was the organ of the Latter Day Saints' church. It will come as no surprise, then, that its news and editorial columns trumpeted support for the church and its positions. Territorial officers and their actions were routinely criticized, as was the federal government. One subject dominated the newspaper's pages and that subject was polygamy. Or, as the Mormons often called it, "plural marriage," or "celestial marriage."

Congress for years had passed laws forbidding the practice, with each new bill imposing ever more severe punishments and sanctions for infractions. The most recent, the Poland Act, as I understood it from the newspapers, more or less removed all Mormon influence from the courts by giving jurisdiction for all criminal and civil justice to the United States district courts.

The Mormon newspaper claimed the Poland Act, like the laws that preceded it, violated the constitutional right of the Saints to practice their religion as they saw fit. The *Tribune* claimed it necessary, as the Latter Day Saints ignored the laws against polygamy and manipulated the justice system to avoid enforcement. Under federal control, the courts had started jailing Mormon men who married more than one woman.

As for me, I would be happy to find one woman with a room to rent. But I did not find her that day. And so, I strapped on my snake leg and stumped out to find supper.

Afterward, I made my way a few blocks south down Main Street to a section known as "Whiskey Street" for all the saloons lining both sides of the road. I took my pick from among the drinking establishments and slipped into O'Malley's Saloon.

As a stranger, I carried no stigma as an undertaker and was free to mingle with other drinkers should I so choose. But as I have mentioned on other occasions, I imbibe but little and am not naturally sociable, and so, by habit, found an empty table in a dim corner at the back of the long, narrow room.

It was there, in the dark recesses of O'Malley's, that I first made the acquaintance of Porter Rockwell.

CHAPTER EIGHTEEN

The beer in my glass fell but an inch over the quarter hour I nursed it, undisturbed. Then the door opened away up at the front and a man came in. He "howdied" the drinkers at the bar and tables, and the few card players surrounding green felt as he limped toward the back. He had no sooner sat down at the next table than O'Malley's bar girl put a schooner of beer and shot of whiskey in front of him. He raised the glass in a toast to the woman.

"Wheat!" he said, and swallowed the whiskey. "I'll have another, if you will, Miss Brady," handing the glass to her.

She smiled and walked away and the man turned his attention my way. He nodded a head framed by long tresses, longer than any I've ever seen on a man. A beard, as grizzled and grayshot as his hair, fell to the middle of his barrel chest. He was broad, but not fat, and looked to be as solid as a hickory stump.

I acknowledged his nod with one of my own and said, "Wheat?"

He raised his glass and gulped down half his beer. "Wheat," he said in his high-pitched voice. "It's what's left when you separate the tares, as it says in the Good Book somewheres. Winnow out the chaff and trash and what you've got is wheat — all the good and none of the bad."

"An interesting expression for a toast."

"It's served me well, all these years."

Miss Brady arrived with his ordered whiskey, but he let it rest on the tabletop and looked me over. "A stranger, you are."

"Yes. New in town." I handed him a calling card and he studied it.

"Miss Brady!" The barmaid came back and he handed her the card. "What does it say, gal?"

She tilted the card back and forth until enough of the dim light struck it to allow her to read aloud, "Jonathon 'Pinebox' Collins, Undertaker and Embalmer." She looked me over, handed him the card, and went back up front. The man studied the card again then slipped it into a pocket of his vest.

"A corpse doctor, are you?"

"That I am, although not practicing the

trade at present."

"Oh? What is it you're practicin'?"

"I've just taken a job with a cabinetmaker. Alonzo Hadley. Do you know him?"

" 'Lonzo? Sure I do. Known ol' 'Lonzo a good long time. Fine man. Nails up a fine cabinet, too."

"It appears so, from what I saw in his shop. My woodworking abilities don't measure up to his, but he seems to think I can be of help."

The man swallowed another mouthful of beer and belched. "What is it they call you? Pinebox, like it says on that there card?"

"Some do."

He smiled. "I like it. That's what I'll call you. Pinebox."

"And what shall I call you?"

He took another swallow from his beer before answering. "Most folks call me 'Port.' I reckon you may as well, too."

"As you wish, Port." I held my glass toward him. "Wheat," I said and he laughed as I took a sip. "What do you do, Port, if you don't mind my asking?"

"Oh, this 'n' that. Got some business interests here in town. Own the Colorado Stables over the way," he said with a nod in what I assumed to be the direction of the place. "Got a hotel and brewery down by the point of the mountain. Run ranches out west on Government Creek and down in Juab County. Horses, mostly. Some cattle."

He drained off the last of his beer and called for Miss Brady to bring another. The whiskey glass sat, still full. After a long draught from his fresh beer he said, "Of late, last few years, I been in a place called Grass Valley. South of here, it is. Near 'bout two hundred miles, I reckon. Sent down there by Brother Brigham, tryin' to get a town goin'. It's a nice enough place, but it's good to be home. Man my age likes a chance to take his ease when he can. Damn hard work, makin' a settlement."

"Sounds like you're a busy man."

"Only when I can't help it. Like I said, a man my age . . ."

He drifted away in thought, and so I let him go. After a few minutes he drank his beer then picked up the whiskey and held it up in a toast to no one in particular. "Wheat!" he said, and drank it off all at once.

"Nice to meet you, Pinebox," he said as stood.

"The pleasure is mine, Port." I watched him limp his way to and out the door.

A man standing at the bar watched him leave, waited a bit, then leaned out the front door and looked down the street. He closed the door, walked to my table and sat down, without invitation, in the chair opposite mine.

"Know who that was you was talkin' to, mister?"

"He said his name is Port."

The man laughed. "It's 'Port' all right. Leastways, that's some of it. Rest of it is Porter Rockwell. Orrin Porter Rockwell."

I'd heard the name, I knew, but it did not register when or why. He took my blank look as an invitation to inform me.

"Porter Rockwell. Man's a killer. Hell, he'd as soon shoot a man as look at him."

I mulled that over. "He seems a friendly enough fellow."

"Might do. But that don't change a thing. He's been spillin' blood all the way from the California goldfields to the Mississippi River and ever'wheres in between these past . . . must be thirty, thirty-five years."

"The name does seem familiar, but only just."

"Well, he's old. Semi-retired from the killin' business, they say. But he'll still kill a man if Brigham Young says so."

"I've known a few gunmen in my time. Buried a number of them, as it happens.

Not many live to be as old as Port looks to be."

The man laughed. "Oh, you can't kill Porter Rockwell. He's protected by God his own self, they say."

I asked what he meant and he launched into a meandering tale about Rockwell and his friend Joseph Smith, who started the church of the Latter Day Saints and ran it until he was killed back in Illinois. It seems Port was arrested and jailed in Missouri for the better part of a year. Locked him up on suspicion of the attempted murder of Lilburn Boggs, former governor of that state, who was behind the Mormons being run out of there.

But Rockwell was turned loose for lack of evidence and made his way to Nauvoo, in Illinois, where Joseph and his people had resettled. He had to sneak out of Missouri, avoiding those who wanted to kill him — likely most everyone in the state — and arrived in Nauvoo with the dirt and stink of the Missouri jail still on him, including unkempt hair and beard that hadn't seen the benefit of soap or scissors for all those months.

As the story goes, the man told me, Joseph put Port to work as his bodyguard and enforcer, pronouncing a prophecy on his head that if he never cut his hair or beard he would be protected, spared from death or even wounding by any opponent.

"Surely no one believes that," I said.

"Oh, hell yes. Rockwell himself lives by it. All these Mormons swear by it, too. They'll tell you story after story 'bout how bullets bounce off him and other such nonsense. But, there ain't no disputin' the fact that he's killed forty, maybe fifty men in gunfights or by ambush — some say he's killed lots more than that — and he ain't never took a bullet himself.

"Just lucky, maybe. But who am I to say? All I know is, he's a murderin' sonofabitch and you had best walk softly 'round him 'less you want to end up worm food. You bein' an undertaker and all, accordin' to that barmaid over there, you know what I mean by that."

He stood, reset the hat on his head, and walked out of O'Malley's Saloon, never to be seen again by me. I don't know who he was, or why he saw fit to warn me. But if he meant to frighten me, his words had the opposite effect. I was intrigued by Porter Rockwell, and hoped for an opportunity to further my acquaintance with him.

The next morning found me standing in front of Alonzo Hadley's cabinet shop, waiting to start the day. Alonzo, no early riser I would learn, showed up half an hour or so later to unlock the door.

"Ready to go to work, are you, Brother Collins — or should I call you Brother Pine-box?"

"As you wish, sir. I'm ready."

Alonzo closed the door behind us. "No need to show up so early for work. I wait till the sun is well up and in the windows. Don't have to light lanterns, that way. What with all the sawdust in the air at times, the place could easily catch fire. Go up like an inferno, if it did."

The morning was an education. Brother Hadley shepherded me from workbench to workbench — some set up with vices and clamps and such to hold work — around the perimeter of the shop. Most of the tools were familiar to my experience. But where I got by with one simple crosscut saw, here there were also rip saws, bucksaws, bow saws, tenon saws, dovetail saws, keyhole saws, coping saws.

My acquaintance with a plane — which I learned was a "trying" plane — paled when introduced to scrub planes, jack planes, coffin planes, fore planes, joiner planes, rebate planes, and molding planes. There were braces and bits, hand drills, and gimlets to make holes. Many kinds of chisels. Froes, drawknives, spokeshaves. Calipers and squares and gauges and other tools for measuring and fitting. Hammers. Mallets. There was a foot-powered grinding stone, and oil stones and whet stones for sharpening tools.

With my brain already spinning, Brother Hadley gave it another whirl when he showed me his lathe. I had heard of the machine, and seen the results of its work, but had never laid eyes on one. It sat propped up on legs, at a height comfortable for a man standing. Running between the legs, about waist high and tipped at an angle to shed the "swarf," or wood shavings, was what he called the bed. Hooked to the bed was an adjustable "banjo" to which was attached a vertical tool post, and to that, a horizontal tool rest. The business end was called the headstock, which had a spindle where the piece of wood to be worked fit. Then you slid the tailstock into position to hold the wood in place. Pumping a treadle with one foot set the spindle and wood to spinning so you could work it over with gouges, chisels, parting tools, skews, and scrapers as appropriate to the job.

If I seem to go on at too much length about Alonzo's lathe, it is only because I found it fascinating. Turning a rough piece of square lumber into a table leg, a spindle for a chair back, pull knobs for a drawer, finials, newel posts, balusters seemed magical.

I even found myself imagining fancy and fanciful peg legs made beautiful by turning on the lathe.

Alas, it was not the lathe at which Alonzo put me to work following my introduction to the shop and its tools. Instead, I was handed a rip saw and set to cutting long, wide boards into long, narrow boards in preparation for Brother Hadley's next project, the nature of which I was not privy to. Upon completion of that job, I was handed a sheet of glasspaper and a block and told to smooth the surfaces of a simple chest of drawers nearly ready for a first coat of varnish.

Along about midafternoon the door opened. I assumed it would be Alonzo's wife Emma with dinner basket in hand.

I was half-right.

There was a dinner basket, all right, but in the hands of a young woman — younger than myself, I judged, no more than twenty years if that. Her dress was much like those seen everywhere on the streets of the city: simple, plain, and cut to conceal the wear-er's feminine form. Like Emma the day before, she wore an apron and a bonnet. But the bonnet served little purpose, as it hung down her back, tied at the neck by its strings. Hair the color of corn silk gathered in a thick braid and fairly glowed in the afternoon light filtered through dusty windows. She passed by with a nod, the hint of a smile in eyes the color of the top of the sky.

The young woman talked quietly with Alonzo for a moment, set the dinner basket on his workbench, and left. I realized my hand, stilled upon the top of the chest, had not moved since first I saw her.

Alonzo invited me over to his workbench, and as he rifled through the basket choosing what to eat from a selection of foodstuffs, I took dry sandwiches from the flour sack a hash house near the Farnham Hotel had wrapped them in, and we ate.

Not wishing to appear nosy, I did not ask about the young woman, but he said between bites of a fat pickle, "That was my Hulda, by the way."

I only nodded as I chewed. After a few minutes of silence, save the sounds of eating, I said, "I met a friend of yours last evening."

"Oh? Who might that be?"

"Port, he called himself. I was told his full name is Porter Rockwell."

Alonzo chewed on the news for a while. "Hmm. Port's back in town, is he? I thought he was down south somewhere on a mission for Brother Brigham."

I nodded. "He said so — said he had been, anyway. Said he was glad to be back home in town."

With a smile, Brother Hadley said, "Home? Port's home for as long as I've known him has been in the saddle. Maybe the seat of a wagon. He's on the move more than he ever sits still. The brethren have had him up to all manner of things. Carried the mail, he did, when it was dangerous. Ran an express business for Brother Brigham. Parleys with the Indians hereabout. He was a territorial marshal — still is, I suppose. He tracks down thieves and rustlers better than any ten men in the Territory — or anywhere else for that matter."

"A man warned me to be careful around him. Said he was a killer."

Alonzo nodded. "He's right. Some of it, anyway. Ol' Port has killed more than his share for certain. Him being an officer of the law — and protector of our prophets — desperate measures have been part of his job and calling. But I do not believe he is a dangerous man by nature. Quite the opposite, in my experience. Always jovial. Willing to share a story and a drink with any man — although I do not hold with his drinking, which is sometimes excessive. That, I am of the opinion, is his greatest sin. And may well prove his downfall."

"How about this business with his hair? How he can't be hurt by his enemies? That true?"

Bother Hadley took half an already-shelled hardboiled egg in one bite and used the time chewing to consider an answer. He swallowed and followed the egg down with cold tea. Then, "I'd have to say time has proved it to be true. Port has been in many a shooting scrape in his time and walked away from every one. Oh, there are ridiculous stories about some of his escapes and I do not give any of them credence. But there have been enough real affrays, attested to by reliable witnesses, to convince me that Brother Rockwell enjoys a kind of divine protection not extended to the rest of us."

Alonzo's explanation made me want all the more to get better acquainted with Porter Rockwell. I could say the same about Hulda Hadley.

Chapter Nineteen

There is plenty of time to think when you spend hour after hour pushing a rebate plane back and forth, cutting rabbet joints on drawer bottoms and sides. I thought about Pioche and the death of Marc Henry; the violence that reigned there and the relative peacefulness of Salt Lake City. I considered The Dismal Trade, and whether or not I would ever again lay out a body. I wondered in the larger sense what the future might bring, and what I might do to meet it.

And that sparked thoughts of Hulda Hadley, and a curiosity concerning her place — or lack of it — in times to come. I had laid eyes on the girl but once since she first came into the shop. That encounter, like the first, was nothing more than an exchange of glances as she passed by on her way to deliver a dinner basket to Alonzo, then half smiles as she left.

Then, early one afternoon, I helped Brother Hadley load a wagon with a high-boy, chest of drawers, and bedstead for delivery to a customer a few miles down the valley in a town called Murray. When Hulda arrived with his dinner basket, I was working over the cutting edge of the blade for a plane on an oil stone. Hulda pulled off her bonnet and let it hang down her back, uncovering her hair, which again hung in a thick braid.

She set the basket on Alonzo's usual work bench and looked around the shop. "Where is Brother Hadley?"

"Left a while ago for Murray. Delivering a bedroom suite." I wiped the oil off my hands and tossed the rag aside, busying myself putting the plane back together, finding it difficult work with trembling hands and uncooperative eyes that preferred looking at the girl.

Hulda thought for a moment, then dragged a stool near and sat down, sweeping her dress against the back of her thighs as she did. "How are you enjoying our city?"

"It's a lovely place. Much nicer than where I last lived."

"Oh? And where was that? If you do not mind saying."

"Pioche."

"That is in Nevada, is it not? A place where they have mines?"

"Yes. Yes, it is."

"There are mines here, too. In Park City, and Alta. Bingham Canyon, too. But Brother Brigham does not approve much of mining."

"Why is that?"

Hulda bowed her head and smoothed the apron across her lap as she thought. "He believes, I think, that pursuit of riches for their own sake is sinful, and that gold and silver turn men's heads and distract them from their first duty."

"And what might that be?"

"Building Zion."

My expression betrayed my ignorance.

"Building the Kingdom of God on Earth. Preparing for Jesus Christ's second coming. To do so, we need people. Families. From what I hear the brethren say, that is becoming more difficult with the United States government persecuting us because of our desire to do so according to the tenets of our religion."

"You mean men having more than one wife."

She nodded.

"And what do you think of it?"

Huldah shrugged. "It is the way of things.

The brethren say it is the Lord's will."

"What do the women say?"

She shrugged again and ducked her head, looking at me through long eyelashes. "As for us, the women, obedience to the priesthood is expected. That is all there is to it." Looking away, she clasped her hands in her lap, interlacing the fingers. She looked up after a moment. "Tell me what happened to your leg."

My response started out simple enough, but Hulda's questions turned it into a lengthy recounting of my life since leaving the farm in Claryville, Kentucky. Unlike most folks in my experience, she seemed ambivalent about my work as an undertaker. Her interest in my peg leg was mere curiosity rather than the mild revulsion of so many. She even seemed slightly amused at the snake coiled around my shin.

"Oh my!" she said, noticing the angle of light through the windows. "I have frittered away the most of the afternoon! I must get home and help Mother Emma with supper." On the way to the door she pulled on her bonnet. She opened the door and turned back to me. "I have enjoyed our talk, Brother Collins."

"Please — call me Jon. Or Jonathon. Or Pinebox, if you'd rather."

She smiled. "Good day to you, then, Brother Pinebox." Hulda closed the door behind her leaving, leaving only the echo of her cerulean eyes.

I worked the plane steadily through what remained of the afternoon, attempting to catch up the lost progress. Alonzo returned just after I finished and found me readying to close down the shop. He examined my work and found it acceptable and went to tidy up his workbench.

"Ah — my dinner! I must have forgotten to tell Emma I would not need it this day."

"Hulda brought it by. She was surprised to not find you here."

Alonzo shook his head with a tsk-tsk clicking of his tongue. "I fear I am getting forgetful. I must remember to apologize when I get home — if I don't forget to do so," he said with a chuckle.

My day proved doubly blessed in its encounters when I stopped by O'Malley's Saloon. I hobbled my way to the back of the room and there at a corner table sat the other Mormon I wished to know better: Porter Rockwell.

"Pinebox Collins, if I ain't mistook. Pull up a chair and I'll treat you to a glass of this watery brew O'Malley passes off as beer."

"I heard that, Port!" O'Malley hollered from up front. "Mind how you talk. What if I told you the barrels from which I draw my lager come from your own Hot Springs Brewery?"

"I'd say you was a liar, which I know to be true. This piss came from Dick Margetts's Utah Brewery sure as I'm sittin' here."

O'Malley laughed. "I wouldn't lie to you, Port. It's from the Utah, all right. But I never lied. You'll recall I said, 'What if I told you.' So, I never said it was Hot Springs beer."

This time Port laughed. "O'Malley, you're better at not sayin' what you mean than I am, and that's sayin' something."

As before, a shot glass of whiskey sat beside Rockwell's schooner of beer. Miss Brady delivered a glass dripping foam to me, and a fresh, full beer to Port. He swallowed what was left of the first glass and swiped his mouth and mustaches with the back of his hand. "I never knowed from before that you had but the one leg, Pinebox. How did that come to be?"

I told my well-rehearsed story of the Battle of Hartsville and how one of Colonel John Hunt Morgan's cannonballs took my foot and ankle while I was yet half-asleep. "I notice you, yourself, walk with a limp, Port. How did that come to be? If you don't mind saying."

"Nah. It don't make no never mind to me. I been hobblin' along on this poor prop most all my life. Broke it when I was but a little shaver back in New York and it never got set right. Ain't worked proper since — a mite shorter than the other'n, it is. Pains me more in my old age than it used to — makes sittin' a saddle for any length of time a trial." He paused to make a dent in the new glass of beer. "Still and all, I get by. As do you, it appears. Show me that there peg leg of yours. It looks to be somethin' more than a post."

Further amusement and conversation followed the revelation of my snake. And Rockwell was likewise tickled when I told him of my former appendage in the shape of a steer's leg.

"Bein' a cow man myself, I would dearly love to see that one. You still use it?"

"Afraid not. A bullet took a big chunk out of it, and so I retired it."

"Bullet? You shoot the sonofabitch who shot you?"

I explained the circumstances of the shooting, and how the man whose bullet hit my leg was more or less dead when he fired the shot.

"Pioche, eh? I've heard tell that's a rough place. From what I hear, there's more lead in the air than silver in the ground."

"That could well be true. I saw more gunfights and killing and I laid out more men who died from being shot than I care to remember. Much worse than Abilene with all its Texas cowboys. I got used to seeing shot-up bodies at the army hospitals in Nashville. But that was war, and you expected it. Pioche, though, all that killing was unnecessary — nothing but avarice behind it. Still going on, I expect."

Rockwell sat silent, swirling the beer in his glass before gulping it down. "Killin' ain't never pleasant. But there's times when it's got to be done."

"Meaning no disrespect, sir, but I have been told you have killed a number of men."

"Who told you that?"

"I don't know. A man here at the saloon, after we last talked. And Alonzo Hadley, he told me you have shot men in the line of duty. As a deputy marshal, I believe he said."

"Ain't no sense denyin' it. I have lived through violent times, and I've lived through it on account of me bein' handier with a gun than them that wanted to kill me. Plenty of times, just bein' a Mormon was reason enough to get killed. Now that the damn government is startin' to lock up men for nothin' more than them havin' wives, there might be blood spilled ag'in."

"Do you think so?"

He shrugged. "Don't know. Depends on what Brother Brigham says and what the federal marshals do. They go after Brigham, like some say they're bound to do, they'll have to go through me to get to him."

"But aren't you a federal marshal yourself?"

"Guess so. I was made one years ago and ain't never been told I ain't. Still got the badge. Them *federales* runnin' the show around here don't claim me, I know that. But come down to it, I was a Mormon 'fore I was a marshal, and it'll stay that way."

We sipped our beer in silence for a while. Or, it would be more correct to say, I sipped at mine and Rockwell swallowed his in long draughts and emptied his glass, then lowered another to a level below mine before we resumed talking.

I swallowed hard before asking my next question. "Meaning no disrespect, Port, I am told you spent time in jail."

He laughed, but without humor. "You been told that, have you. Well, what else was you told about that?"

"I was not given much in the way of detail. Something about the shooting of the governor of Missouri."

Again he laughed. "Oh, that time. Let my guard down and paid for it, I did. A pair of damn bounty men saw me walk off a riverboat in St. Louis and nabbed me. Hauled me to Independence where that sonofabitch of a sheriff J. H. Reynolds throwed me in his pisshole of a jail and kept me there nigh on a year. Him and the judge tried to hang that Boggs shootin' on me but couldn't do it. Finally had to let me go." He stopped to slug down more of his beer and signal for another. "Sonsabitches still claim I did it."

"Did you?"

His stare liked to have stuck me to the back of my chair like an arrow. His light blue eyes turned dark, veiled in shadow as he bowed his head and stared at me from under the wide brim of his hat. "Here's the thing about that. If you think I shot that useless pile of dung they call Lilburn W. Boggs, you'll have to prove it. All the law in Missouri couldn't prove it way back then, and you can't now. Boggs should've died that night like the newspapers said he did. But he didn't. Me or whoever it was tried to kill him should've done a better job on account of he don't deserve to live. I'll brook no more questions from the likes of you about it."

It took me a while to catch my breath. "I'm sorry, Port. I meant no disrespect. Just curious, is all."

Rockwell exhaled a long breath then sat back in his chair. "That's all right, Pinebox. I been asked about Boggs so damn many times just the thought of it gets my blood a-boilin'."

After letting the air clear and temperature drop for a while, I wondered why, being a noted gunfighter and likely the target of young gunslingers wanting to prove themselves, Port was not carrying a gun.

He reached into the pocket of his coat and pulled out what looked to be a Colt revolver. But, unlike others I had seen, the barrel was only about three inches long. "Wouldn't get out of bed without it. Got another one just like it in my other pocket."

I asked about the short barrel.

"Oh, I sawed 'em off. Had a gunsmith do it, should say. That way, they fit in my pocket better and don't get hung up when I need to pull 'em."

"You don't use holsters?"

"Nah. Found 'em uncomfortable when spendin' so much time in the saddle. Long gun is better most times. Shotgun for close work. Still load these pistols with buckshot more often than not. But since I got me a new forty-four Henry rifle — man give it to me in thanks for me retrieving his rustled cattle — I may well get me a new pistol. They make some that shoot the same rim-fire cartridges as the Henry."

"But carrying a pistol in your pocket — isn't that a disadvantage against a man with a holster? Seems like he could get to the gun faster."

A smile and soft chuckle preceded his answer. "If there's one thing I've learned about gunfightin' all these years, it's that most men are in too much of a damn hurry and end up feedin' buzzards for it. I've killed men a lot faster than me by takin' my time and bein' sure of my aim. A man'll live a hell of lot longer by shootin' straight than shootin' fast. Not that you want to dawdle, mind you. Sounds funny to say it, but when you go fast, you want to do it real slow."

He was right. It did sound funny. But I could see the sense of it. It reminded me of Alonzo's advice in the cabinet shop to take your time and let the tools do the work.

"Well, son, it's got late on us and my eyelids is slammin' shut. I'll either have to whittle me some toothpicks to prop 'em open, else wander on up to my room at the

Colorado Stables and go to bed." Port picked up the shot glass and clinked it against my schooner with a smile and a "Wheat!" and so we said our goodnights.

I had no way to know it at the time, but Porter Rockwell would not be as congenial at our next parting.

CHAPTER TWENTY

The block of wood spun on the lathe, responsive to my foot on the treadle. Given the discomfort of standing for long periods on my peg leg, I sat perched upon a tall stool. I switched tools frequently, getting a feel for what each gouge, skew, chisel, and scraper would do as it cuts. I had watched Alonzo at the lathe for hours, and soon came to appreciate how adept he was with the machine. Learning the right combination of speed and pressure, knowing the best gouge to create the desired effect, and feeling the characteristics of the wood would take time and patience and practice.

I put in the time in snatches, whenever there was a spare moment in the shop. And once Alonzo decided I was no longer a danger to myself or the lathe, he gave me a key to the door and allowed me to stay on after hours. Had you asked, I would have sworn on a stack of Bibles that I reduced a full cord of wood to chips and shavings as I practiced turning out flats and fillets and flutes, beads and ogees, V-cuts and swells.

After a time, I became competent, though not accomplished, at turning wood. Visits to some of the city's lumber yards turned up a likely looking piece of seasoned red elm that I thought would make a fine and fancy wooden leg, turned out in the style of a decorative — if overdone — table leg or baluster.

Things slowed down at the shop, and so I had plenty of time to do the job, which I went about at a slow and steady pace. One afternoon while I was at work, Hulda came by with Alonzo's dinner basket then sat and watched while I cut a row of decorative beads along a section of the would-be leg.

"What is it you are making?"

I stopped the treadle with my foot, which in turn stopped the turning of the lathe. "Oh, just trying to make myself more useful around here by learning how to run this contraption. Thought I'd try my hand at a leg, while I was at it."

She laughed. "Quite frilly. You will be doing some fancy footwork with that."

She looked on as I evened out the beads and raised a swell just above them — what would be on top of them with the leg in use. Needing a break — more for fear of fouling up with the distraction of lovely young woman standing nearby than from fatigue — I let the lathe wind down and turned on the stool.

"How are things, Hulda?"

"As well as can be expected for a girl with two ordinary legs."

I smiled at the twinkle in her already-sparkling blue eyes.

We talked of trivial things, laughing together at the slightest hint of humor. Hulda stepped closer to the lathe, brushing against me as she did. Reaching out and running a finger slowly and gently along the peaks and valleys of the emerging leg, she sighed. "It really is beautiful, Brother Pinebox. I cannot wait to see it complete — and in use."

"Hulda!" Alonzo said, then took a bite from a slice of buttered bread. He chewed as Hulda blushed, stepping back and fixing her eyes on the floor as if the wood chips there had something to reveal. "Hadn't you best be getting back home? I'm sure Mother Emma needs your help."

Without looking up, she laid a hand on my arm and turned and walked out of the shop.

Alonzo watched her leave, turned his attention to me for a moment, took another bite of the bread, then turned back to his workbench and gathered the remains of his meal.

A week or so later on a Saturday morning, work was slow and Alonzo had a prospective customer to visit, so he told me to take the afternoon off. I took lunch at a downtown restaurant, then walked out into the streets to have a look around. Dozens of workmen scurried and scrambled about the temple lot, raising inch by inch the elaborate walls of the outsized house of worship. In the next block, armed guards — trying to look inconspicuous but obvious in their duty — loitered around the entrances of the Beehive House and Lion House, where Brigham Young worked and lived. Attempted — and accomplished — arrests of Mormon men "living the principle" of multiple wives had the city on edge. Leaders of the church went about their business discreetly, avoiding public appearances as much as possible.

Across the way on Main Street another construction project had just been finished, and a big new store was now open. The sign above the tall entry doors read, HOLINESS TO THE LORD and ZION COOPERATIVE MERCANTILE INSTITUTION. The Mormon newspaper, the *Deseret Evening News,* hailed the opening as a giant step forward in commerce in the city: a cooperative effort among merchants and manufacturers to provide goods and services at reasonable prices without enriching the "Gentile" retailers with their exorbitant charges. The *Salt Lake Tribune* took a different view, claiming the institution represented nothing more than yet another attempt by the Mormon hierarchy to exert more control over life in Utah Territory at the expense of free enterprise and independence.

I took the opportunity to look the place over to see if it lived up to the publicity, good or bad, in the newspapers. I learned right away from clomping around the several levels of the building on my snake leg that it was even bigger than I imagined. Items on display lined the shelves, allowing customers to handle the goods. Shoes and boots and more shoes and boots, all made in Mormon manufactories, were available. Clothing of all descriptions, from everyday to workwear to finery — albeit rather plain according to modern fashion — was for sale. Housewares, groceries, fabrics, linens, furniture, bedding, tools, seeds, and more. While I don't believe you could buy horses or mules, you could buy harnesses for them and wagons and carriages and farm implements to hitch them to.

Rounding the end of an aisle featuring fruit preserves and canned goods, I pulled up short to avoid bumping into Hulda. She put the can of tomatoes she was studying back on the shelf and smiled. "Why, Brother Pinebox! What an unexpected pleasure!"

"It is good to see you again, Hulda. Are you well?"

"Yes. Yes I am."

Unsure what to say next but wanting to extend the conversation, I invited Hulda to walk with me to the soda fountain at the end of the aisle, with a promise to treat her to an ice cream soda — a popular new delight concocted lately somewhere back east.

We talked and laughed as we spooned and slurped the sweet treats and kept at it long after our glasses were empty. Hulda said she had few opportunities to talk with people near her own age, and our chance meeting was a welcome break from the company of Mother Emma and Alonzo.

No sooner had she said it than Emma spied us from down an aisle. She hooked her shopping basket in the crook of her elbow, hiked up her skirt, and marched toward us, stopping only when hindered by the table at which we sat. I stood and bowed slightly, but Emma did not even look my way.

"Hulda, we are here to do our marketing, not dilly-dally. Say goodbye to Brother Collins."

With that, she turned and marched back down the aisle, never looking back.

"I am sorry, Brother Pinebox. As you see, I must be going." She stood and offered her hand. I reached out and she gave mine a firm squeeze. "Thank you very much for the refreshment."

I watched as she trailed Emma, wondering when next I would have the pleasure of her company. I determined to make it soon.

Alonzo's visit that Saturday resulted in an order for furnishing a kitchen — table, chairs, cabinets — and so Monday morning started a busy week. An examination of my new peg leg, the turning of which I had completed, impressed Alonzo and he assigned me the task of turning the legs for the newly ordered table.

The very thought of turning out four identical pieces taxed my inexperienced mind, so Alonzo sat me down for schooling. He laid out the dimensions of the legs and we selected a suitable piece of wood from the stock. Once I sawed out rough lengths for working and planed them square, he drew out on a piece of scrap lumber his basic design for the features of the legs. I breathed a sigh of relief on seeing he wanted only a gentle swell from a flat and fillet at the bottom to a thick bead and V cut, transitioning to a square top for joining to the tabletop frame.

He had me saw out the one-sided design, saying the resulting "stick" would provide a pattern for turning the first leg, which would serve as the guide for the other three. Still unsure how it would work, I watched Alonzo fasten the first board to the headstock and tailstock on the lathe. He laid his stick against the wood that would become the first leg, marking with pencil where to begin rounding. He started the lathe spinning and used a roughing gouge to cut the corners and round the wood, stopping when it was slightly larger than the thickest part of what would be the finished leg. He had me round the stock for the other legs the same.

Next, Alonzo laid his guide stick against the rounded stock and with a pencil drew a hashmark at each transition: the low point at the bottom of the leg where the swell began, the end of the swell near the top where the bead began, the high point of the bead, the transition point from the bead to the V cut, and the top end of the V. Slowly working the treadle, he laid the pencil against the stock as if it were a tool and watched as each hash mark became a ring around the wounded wood.

"Do you see it now, son? Is it in your mind and hands?"

"I don't know. I think so."

Alonzo laughed. The fancy appendage I had turned lay on a nearby workbench awaiting work on the socket for my stump. "Brother Collins, there is nothing here so intricate as what you cut on this wooden leg of yours."

"True enough. But that didn't have to match anything. I just made it up as I went along."

"Well, just do the best you can. With all the practice you've had on this peg leg and the other pieces you've turned, you will do fine."

And so I pumped away on the treadle and gouged away at the wood, stopping frequently to compare my work to the pattern on the stick, now clamped to the back of the lathe, out of the way but always in sight.

Alonzo examined my work, turning the lathe slowly as he felt along the length of the leg, seeking out any irregularities and finding none. "Fine work, Brother Collins.

You have the knack, I dare say."

"Thank you. But can I do as well on the other three?"

"Easier than you think." He removed the pattern stick from the back of the machine and clamped the emerging table leg in its place. "Use that for your pattern now. And use these." He picked up a set of calipers, one of several pair he had laid on a nearby bench in readiness.

Following his lead, I adjusted other calipers to various places along the leg and set them aside to aid in checking my work as it went along. Alonzo stopped by from time to time to watch over my shoulder and to put the calipers to use. After I finished turning the second leg, he declared it good and said I was on my own with the remaining two legs. When I finished with the turning, he laid the legs out side by side on a bench and looked them over.

"I'm afraid they aren't exact matches," I said.

"They never are. A man's eyes and hands can only do so much. Differences in one piece of the wood from the next will cause variations. The speed of the lathe and sharpness of the tools, as well. But, these look to be as near identical as ever a set of table legs will be." He clapped me on the shoulder. "Now, get to work on the chair legs. Turn enough for six chairs. Front legs and back posts. Sketch yourself out a design similar to the table legs."

The work on the kitchen furniture kept us busy for days. I saw Hulda only once, when she brought Alonzo's dinner basket on a day Mother Emma was busy at something she could not set aside. She said nothing and offered only a sideways glance without moving her bowed head as she left. Somehow, discomfort had replaced our earlier easiness.

I worried about it for a few days before getting up the gumption to act. One evening as we tidied up the shop after a long day of work, I asked Alonzo to sit as I had a question for him.

"And what might that be, Brother Collins?"

"It's Hulda."

He cocked his head and furrowed his eyebrows before saying, "Yes?"

"I have grown somewhat fond of her. I don't know her well, but want to know her better." Once started, I could not stop. "She says she misses the company of people closer to her own age, and we seem to get along well together. I assure you there is nothing dishonorable in my intentions toward her and I promise to treat her with the utmost respect. What I am trying to say, sir, is that I would like your permission to call on your daughter."

Alonzo looked perplexed, then bewildered, and somewhat embarrassed before answering. "I am afraid you have the wrong end of the stick, Brother Collins. Hulda is not my daughter — she is my wife."

CHAPTER TWENTY-ONE

The walls in my room at the Farnham Hotel pressed in more than usual: the confinement painful. The very fact that I was as yet, after all this time in the city, still tucked away in a hotel rather than a boardinghouse or rented room added to my annoyance.

But my every effort to find living quarters in more homelike — and less expensive — quarters came to naught. Oh, there were a few prospects. One widow woman all but promised lodging in a spare room, then reneged upon learning I did not share her Mormon faith. A rooming house on the outskirts of downtown and nearer to Alonzo's shop also denied me a place when they determined I was not a Saint.

I tossed and turned through the night in the tight quarters of the Farnham, a place made for brief stays but not for living. Even my cramped quarters in Pioche came with meals of a sort, sparing me the expense of paying restaurant prices for every meal.

Adding to my anxiety, causing the most of it as a matter of fact, was Alonzo's revelation about Hulda. Why, here in Salt Lake City among the polygamous Mormons, it had not occurred to me she was spouse rather than daughter is a mystery. Her age, I suppose. Her calling Emma "Mother Emma" — a common appellation, I learned later, for the first wife and mother — may have affected my thinking.

Still and all, the very notion of such a lovely, spirited young woman as Hulda bound to an old man like Alonzo — fine man though he may be — turned my stomach.

The future of my relationship with Alonzo contributed to my late-night angst. I liked the man. I enjoyed working with him. He had taught me much, and I had much more to learn. I found the work appealing. Many an undertaker came to The Dismal Trade through cabinetry — their building of coffins led to laying out the bodies to fill them as part of the natural course of things. That I was taking that path in the opposite direction also seemed natural, somehow.

But what would Alonzo's attitude be toward me now that he knew I had feelings for Hulda? Would he accept it as a simple misunderstanding? Or would he fear the attraction would continue despite my knowing the truth of the matter? Or would he send me packing?

To my surprise, Alonzo acted as if our uncomfortable conversation never happened. We went about our work in the shop in the usual manner, crafting and assembling the parts and pieces of the kitchen furnishings, along with other small projects that came along.

If Alonzo appeared content to forget about my infatuation with his wife, I was not. If part of my desire to keep company with Hulda had been giving her respite from a restrictive life with strait-laced Mormon parents, the actual facts of her situation made rescue more pressing than mere respite.

But did Hulda need, or even want, rescue? She had seemed resigned to plural marriage in earlier conversations, but I had interpreted that resignation as something she may face in the future. Did it matter that she was more lively, more vivid, more lovely when we were together? Or did her commitment to Mormonism and "priesthood" rule matter more?

I determined that the only way to know was to ask Hulda.

The opportunity did not soon present itself. Day after day, it was Emma who brought Alonzo his dinner. Evenings spent lurking around the streets in her neighborhood — attempting to do so inconspicuously but perhaps failing — and hoping to find her out and about were futile.

Then one morning Alonzo mentioned in passing that Emma was feeling poorly. On the off chance her malady might continue until time to bring Alonzo his dinner spurred me to tear a blank sheet from the back of the book tucked away in my lunch bag and pencil a note in hope of passing it to Hulda should she come.

When she opened the door and stepped through, pulling her bonnet back and uncovering her thick, glowing, braided hair, I feared Alonzo would hear my pounding heart over the sound of the tap-tap-tap of his mallet as he tested the fit of mortise-and-tenon joints. With the folded note in hand, I carried the chairback I had just assembled across the room to stow it with its mates at a place where Hulda would pass as she left.

And so we met that Saturday afternoon in a quiet, out-of-the-way café frequented mostly by the Gentiles of the city. I begged off work, telling Alonzo I needed the afternoon to continue my fruitless search for better lodgings. What Hulda told Emma, I do not know. Tentative and suspicious upon entering, she brightened when I pulled out a chair at the table I had chosen against the back wall.

We talked over slices of apple pie. Hulda allowed as how she enjoyed my company, even hinted at some romantic interest. I confessed my affection for her and my desire to continue a relationship, if such were possible under the circumstances, and my willingness to change those circumstances if not.

"Oh, Pinebox. I do not know how either of those things could be possible. The church leaders gave me to Alonzo in marriage and that is the way it is."

"But it doesn't have to be that way. We can leave here. Go elsewhere and make a new life."

"The thought of a life with you is intriguing — that is for certain. But what of my life here? What of my family? Not Alonzo and Mother Emma, but my father and mother who came from the old country to live with the Saints; what of my brothers and sisters?"

Hulda admitted she was not as committed to Mormon teachings as some, and that she bridled at the expectation of unquestioning obedience. But, still, she was unsure about leaving the only life she had known. As I scraped the last remnants of pie from my plate with the side of my fork, Hulda said she would consider going away with me but made no promises. I pressed on.

"I don't have much to offer, I know. But we can make a life. I could hire on with a cabinetmaker somewhere, maybe open my own shop. Or, I can always take up undertaking again."

Hulda smiled. "I do not imagine you would ever want for work as an undertaker. People will never stop dying." She squeezed my hand, smiled again, and left. The thought of our next meeting already brightened my thoughts.

Come Monday, Alonzo seemed distant and preoccupied but said nothing. He was never talkative, so his deeper silence did not concern me overmuch. For the most part, we went about our work same as always. When he called it a day, I stayed on and completed the work on my fancy new leg, putting the finishing touches on the fit of the socket and adjusting the padding. Evenings over the course of the week found me applying varnish, then attaching leather straps and belts, creating the harness to hold it in place while in use.

Saturday evening found me stumping along Whiskey Street in my new appendage and into O'Malley's Saloon. I made my way through the long, narrow room to my accustomed place in the back, beyond the scant crowd and brighter lights. I sat down and ordered a beer from Miss Brady and had barely sipped the foam off the top when Porter Rockwell walked in.

"Pinebox Collins! May I sit?"

"Sure. I'll buy you a beer."

"I thank you, son. Don't forget a shot of whiskey to plow a furrow down my throat for that beer to follow, Miss Brady."

We exchanged further pleasantries while the barmaid fetched his drinks. He hoisted the shot glass with his customary toast, "Wheat!" and downed the whiskey in one long gulp.

"How's things at Alonzo's?"

"Fine. Busy."

"He treatin' you all right?"

I nodded, wondering about his concern.

"Word is you was mistook about his Hulda."

Again I nodded.

"I can see why. She's a handsome young woman. Ain't no man alive wouldn't give her a second look."

I did not nod that time. I stared into my schooner wondering what would come next.

Rockwell smiled and I breathed easier. He said, "What did Alonzo have to say about it?"

"I guess he was as surprised as I was, I think — only in a different way. I was shaken to learn she was his wife and he was shocked to learn I thought she was his daughter."

Mulling that over, he swallowed a long draught of his beer, half emptying the glass, signaling the barmaid for another, and another shot of whiskey. "How did you two leave it?"

I did not know how to answer. After what seemed several minutes of tense silence, I said, "Alonzo never said anything, really. Nothing more was ever said."

"He likely thought you'd leave it alone."

I nodded.

Port let that sink in until the silence again grew uncomfortable. "So why didn't you?"

If he did not notice my distress, it was because he was throwing back the rest of his beer. Miss Brady swept by, dropping Rockwell's shot of whiskey and fresh beer on the table, scooping up his empty glasses, and breezed away.

I attempted a sip of my beer to gain time

to collect my thoughts, but my hand trembled so that I set the schooner back down. "What do you mean?"

"I mean your meetin' Hulda Hadley in that there café."

My eyes widened and I could feel the color leach from my face.

"You both had apple pie. You cleaned up your plate. Hulda left the browned edge of the crust on hers. You had coffee. And unless I'm mistook, she had tea."

After staring at Rockwell for a moment I found my voice. "How do you know that?"

He chuckled, albeit so quietly I barely heard. "Pinebox, you been in this city long enough you ought to know there ain't nothin' happens here that them that's runnin' the church don't know about it. Brother Brigham's got his eyes on ever'thing."

"What am I to do?"

"I can't tell you what to do, Pinebox. But let me tell you a little story. Some twenty or so years back there was some soldiers came here — Steptoe's army, we called them, on account of they was led by a Colonel Edward Steptoe. Came here to investigate Indians killing some other army men that had been out here on a survey. Some in the States blamed the Saints for the killings, of course.

"Anyway, things went along fine for a while. Then them soldiers, mostly bein' young men full of piss and vinegar, started lookin' for female company and got to lurin' away our young women. Some of them young women bein' already married, like Hulda. One of them girls that took up with a soldier was married to one of Brother Brigham's boys.

"Now, Brother Brigham, he don't take too kindly to Gentiles messin' with Mormon women. 'Specially them as is in his own family. He all but ordered me to put that particular soldier under. Never happened, as the army left shortly. But I had my eye on that there soldier boy and he wasn't long for this world had he stuck around.

"Thing is, Pinebox, I sorta like you. And it would pain me some if we should come to a disagreement over your intentions where young Hulda is concerned. For if we was to come to a disagreement, I can guaran-damn-tee you'd come off second best. If wind of you gettin' up to anything more with that lass of Alonzo's should make its way to Brother Brigham, an undertaker will likely be needed — only this time, you'll be on the receivin' end of the job."

His light blue eyes fixed on mine as if looking into my mind to see if his words were getting through. "I've heard Brig give this piece of advice from time to time, and you'd be smart if you was to take it. He says, 'A word to the wise is sufficient.' "

Rockwell let that mull while he drained off the rest of his beer, then hoisted the whiskey glass toward me. "Wheat!" he said, and poured it down, then hobbled his way out of O'Malley's.

Port hadn't even noticed my fancy new leg.

were actually brought. Two faded lines also this time, so about four lines to three, the good humored custom is to thank the Lord. I went to shake the Ns ruling sum Dead.. at... their pull stick her shout at the back of the hear, men mushed th.. stalled and pointed down they nodded the way toward LOW lleys.

CHAPTER TWENTY-TWO

As the train rolled into the station at Cheyenne, I tucked my railroad ticket stub between the pages to mark my place in *Around the World in Eighty Days* by Jules Verne. I did not remember Cheyenne from my passage through here in the opposite direction a few years ago. Must have been asleep. Or perhaps absorbed in a book. I had no reason to be here now, other than the fact that Cheyenne was not Salt Lake City. Beyond that, I figured the eastern edge of Wyoming Territory was far enough away that it might put me beyond the grasp of the Mormons, should they decide my "sin" merited further attention.

And, I had nowhere else to be.

I stood around on the railroad platform with carpetbag in hand waiting for the baggage handlers to fetch my trunk and tool bag and a recently acquired case added to hold my growing heap of worldly goods.

Much of what it held wasn't worth the freight. But I had chosen not to take the time in Salt Lake City to sort it all out, preferring instead to get out of town as soon as possible.

My only regret was leaving without saying goodbye to Hulda Hadley, but perhaps it was better this way. Perhaps not. In either case, it was all behind me now and I would have to make the best of it.

A man sitting on a delivery wagon at the end of the platform while his dray was loaded recommended Dyer's Hotel as an economical place to stay and offered to drop me and my trappings at the front door. His kindness likely stemmed from pity for a man with a wooden leg — never mind that the leg was fancier and more intricately turned than any stick of wood he'd ever laid eyes on.

Cheyenne was a scar scratched into the high plains and little more. As far as the eye could see, the world was the color of dust. If there was tree in the city it had not reached sufficient height to show. Even the prairie grass was dun-colored, any green it once carried bleached away in the harsh sunlight. Or, perhaps, stripped by the wind that had not abated since I stepped off the train, and judging from the trash drifted against the buildings, seldom did.

The desk clerk at Dyer's Hotel studied my signature in the register. "And how long will you be staying with us, Mister Collins?"

Since I had only just lifted nib from paper, the man had obviously perfected the art of reading upside down. I stuck the pen back in its holder. "Can't say. Let's make it a week for the time being."

"As you wish."

"Tell me. Where might a man find a meal at a reasonable price?"

He smiled. "Why, Mister Collins we have just such an establishment right here in the hotel. I'm confident you'll find our 'Tin Restaurant' to your liking."

"Tin Restaurant?"

His smile got wider. "An affectionate name. Officially, it's 'Dyer's Restaurant' but in days past, Mister Dyer served meals on cheap tinware. Cowboys gave it the name and it stuck. But the food was good and business was brisk, and the table settings have since been elevated to the finest bone china."

"Does the food taste any better?"

The desk clerk's smile faded. He turned the register around on its turntable. "I can assure you, sir, that I hear no complaints about the food. It is wholesome and as toothsome as any in the Territory."

"I meant no offense, mister —"

"Zane. Will Zane."

"— Zane. Merely an observation that I have, in my travels, had occasion to frequent restaurants whose fixtures and furnishings — and prices — overshadow the quality of the food. On the other hand, I have enjoyed many a fine meal at a sensible price in eateries of the 'tin plate' variety."

"No offense taken, then. I believe we still have a stack of those old tin plates in a cupboard somewhere if you'd prefer to eat off them."

This time, I smiled. "No thank you, Mister Zane. I'm sure your china plates will be more than adequate to their purpose."

And they were. The meals on the chalkboard were simple. The pot roast with gravy I chose was tender and tasty, the buttered parsnips and glazed carrots not yet cooked to mush as was often the case, and the bread pudding and coffee proved a relaxing way to finish off the supper.

"Your recommendation was much appreciated," I said to Will Zane, stopping by the desk to fetch my room key. "The meal was worthy of a china plate, but the price was in keeping with its tin plate origins."

"I'm glad you enjoyed it, Mister Collins."

"As you know, I am new in town. And I am somewhat at loose ends at present and looking for a new prospect."

"You'll be heading north, then. Everyone else is."

"North?"

"Deadwood. The Black Hills. For months now, Cheyenne has been nothing more than a way station for people afflicted with gold fever."

"Ah, yes. I have read of the gold rush in the Black Hills. Aren't there Indian difficulties there?"

"Have been. Can't blame the Sioux — government treated to keep white folks out of the Black Hills in '68, but prospectors wandered in and out anyway — them that weren't killed. Then Custer and his soldiers went in there in '74 and found gold, and even more white men went in. The sourdoughs dodged Indians — again, those who weren't killed — till the big find in Deadwood. By then, Custer was done away with and Crook chased the Sioux and Cheyenne till they scattered. Still, plenty of miners get killed, so they say, but it's other miners killing them. Being in Deadwood isn't good for a man's health, it would seem."

"I have had my fill of mining towns. They do seem to attract violent types."

Zane laughed. "You understate the case, Mister Collins. Deadwood has attracted nothing but riff-raff." He sighed. "But, the excitement there got Wild Bill and his ilk out of Cheyenne, so there is that."

My intake of breath mirrored his sigh. "Wild Bill? You mean Wild Bill Hickok?"

"The same. He was a guest here for some time. Why? Do you know him?"

"As a matter fact I do."

"He a friend of yours?"

"Of sorts. More an acquaintance, really."

"Well, you missed him, but only just. He's gone from here, and good riddance. Went with that circus train of Colorado Charley Utter's when it left here two, maybe three weeks ago. I only wish even more of the gun-toting gamblers and pistoleros and other lowlifes had gone with him."

We talked a while longer about Cheyenne. Zane pointed out an alcove off the lobby where a row of shelves held stacks and stacks of the local newspapers, going back years. He allowed the piles were seldom disturbed, but guests were welcome to relax and read to their hearts' content. I told him I would likely take up the offer, but for now it was off to bed to rest up from my long, monotonous ride on the wearisome rails.

I slept deep and undisturbed save one

247

interruption caused by gunfire in the street related to goings-on at McDaniel's Theatre across the way. "Theatre" it was called, and there were performances there of a sort, as I would later learn, but not the sort of dramatics involving actors and recitations. Scantily clad women, on stage and off, were but another means of separating customers from the contents of their wallets in the drinking and gambling parlors inside McDaniel's.

If I found many of the patrons of McDaniel's and the Senate Saloon and other such establishments reminiscent of the Texas cowboys I had encountered in Abilene, it is because many of them were. Cheyenne was cattle country, with numerous ranches sprawling in every compass point from the town. Tens of thousands of Texas cattle stocked the ranges, delivered to Cheyenne by the same sort of Lone Star drovers who frequented Abilene and other Kansas railhead towns in years past.

Those cowboys, however, went back to Texas after blowing off steam built up over the weeks on the trail. In Cheyenne, many stayed, hired by the ranches to ride herd on the four-legged, grass-eating, money-making machines they trailed here. Big business, the ranches were, more often than not investment properties funded by capitalists from Edinburgh, London, Boston, New York, and other moneyed metropolises.

This and a wealth of other information concerning the capital of Wyoming Territory came to me courtesy of Russel Pomeroy, proprietor of an undertaking and embalming parlor I encountered while strolling the city streets the day after my arrival.

"Time was, Cheyenne was a home of sorts to a lot more people. Some six thousand souls at one time. Can't be more than four thousand nowadays. And it ain't the kind of decline in population that's good for business," he told me with a sly smile as we sipped steaming cups of acidy coffee in his cramped office. "Them that didn't pull up stakes after the Union Pacific finished layin' the rails and moved with their construction crews on down the line to the next 'Hell on Wheels' tent town, are now decamping in droves for Deadwood and other points north."

Once he felt I was comfortable in his presence, he inquired about my lost leg and I repeated the oft-told story.

He said, "I've seen my share of men missing limbs — arms and legs both — from fighting in that war. What I ain't never seen is a peg leg the like of that one you're a-wearin'. Fancier than the newel post on a high-rent whorehouse stairway. How'd that come to be?"

I explained my sojourn in the cabinet shop and my reason for taking a respite from the undertaking business.

"A flood, eh? You wouldn't expect that in the Nevada desert."

"It doesn't rain much, but sometimes when it does it makes up for all the dry times. Trouble is, all that rain all at once does more damage than good. That flash flood ripped a hole through that town that won't soon heal. Then again, there's so much money coming out of the ground I suspect they'll rebuild. They did so after the big fire. But it will take time. They can't drive freight wagons into there fast enough to keep up."

"I suspect the same thing is going on up the way in Deadwood."

Pomeroy allowed there were few opportunities in undertaking in Cheyenne at present. "Like I said, the city's growing the opposite direction it should. I doubt it will dwindle away, on account of the railroad. Denver is prospering, mostly on account of the railroad they built to connect to the main line here. And what with all the supplies shipped in here for freighting to Deadwood, shipping is doing fine. Cattle's doing fine. Other than that, there ain't a whole lot happening. You could sure hang up your shingle, but barring a plague or the like, I can't see there being much for you to do."

I asked about finish carpentry, or cabinet making, maybe building coffins.

"Well, Pinebox, houses are sitting empty. Can't think the last time anyone needed one built. Can't say when it comes to furnishings, but it stands to reason the demand wouldn't be much with no building to speak of going on."

Pomeroy stood and invited me to accompany him to the back shop. It was a roomy layout, with two tables served by a single embalming pump positioned between. "Don't know as I have ever needed two tables, outside of one time I got two victims of a gunfight outside the Senate Saloon. Cowboy from one of the ranches out Chugwater way accused a gambler of cheating. Barkeep told them to take it outside. Gambler put a bullet in the cowboy's right lung, but he managed to shoot the cardsharp in the head before he fell. Damndest thing — ain't never heard of both men in a gunfight killing each other. But here's what I wanted you to see."

He pulled back a curtain that opened onto a room no more than six feet across, but running the length of the wall. Propped upright against the wall stood a row of six coffins. Nothing fancy, just basic burial boxes built to accommodate the average body. "As you see, I have enough pine boxes to meet any demand I'm likely to see in the near future. When I need more, I can get 'em factory-made and shipped in cheap on the railroad."

I left Pomeroy's Undertaking and Embalming Parlor wondering if the absence of opportunities in The Dismal Trade bothered me or not. While I would need work one day, I had sufficient cash laid by from Pioche and Salt Lake City to support me for some time. I made my way back toward Dyer's Hotel intending to spend time with the newspapers hoarded there. Perhaps there would be news of Wild Bill when he hung his hat in Cheyenne.

CHAPTER TWENTY-THREE

Most of the musty, dusty newspapers in their unruly piles in the alcove off the lobby at Dyer's Hotel carried the name *Cheyenne Daily Leader* on the masthead. Scattered among them were copies of what must have been transient publications including the *Cheyenne Daily Tribune* and the *Magic City Record,* along with the more plentiful *Cheyenne Daily Sun.*

Neither rhyme nor reason existed in the stacks, and many of the papers were incomplete, with notices and advertisements torn out and entire pages missing. I suspected there were gaps and absences in chronology as well but had no intention of sorting to prove the thought. I pulled a few newspapers at random from this stack, a few more from that one, and others from another.

Skimming the sheets provided a haphazard glance at matters in Cheyenne over the preceding months and years. Most of what the newspapers reported was of no interest, some stories merited a quick read, other accounts proved engaging. I happened across one narrative of an incident involving Wild Bill Hickok, and the reporting did not flatter the famed gunman.

James Butler "Wild Bill" Hickok, former town tamer turned pistoliferous gambler, who has graced our community with his presence of late, showed his true colors during an unfortunate incident at Boulder's Saloon and Gambling Emporium, on the 17th inst.

Mr. Hickok, upon coming out on the short end of wagering through repeated dealings of the pasteboards, sought to recoup his squandered stakes swiftly by demanding the dealer increase the limits on betting, his assumption being, as is ever the case with cardsharps, that lady luck would favor him in his effort to recover his losses. The house refused to increase the limits, prompting the spurned gambler to assault the proprietor of the card parlor with his walking stick.

The Praetorian Guard on duty at Boulder's failed in their attempts to disarm and dissuade Wild Bill, who held his antagonists at bay with his oft used and much feared nickel plated Colt's revolvers. Mr. Hickok thence swept the pot from the table, added to his purloined refund with a fistful of currency from the cash drawer, pocketed his proceeds, warned off the house bouncers with bloodthirsty threats, and walked unhurriedly out of the gambling parlor and to his lodgings at Dyer's Hotel where, the staff informs us, he retired to his room, from which snoring could be heard to emit mere minutes later.

We can only assume, in light of such nose thumbing at civility and decorum as demonstrated by Wild Bill, that our fair city has abandoned all hope and succumbed to the nefarious natures of Mr. Hickok and his ilk, *nemine contradicente.*

"Nemine contradicente." No one dissenting. Gunslingers such as Wild Bill often ran roughshod over a town, and they sometimes seemed to do so with little or no resistance, or dissent. If one believed the newspaperman, Cheyenne had effectively surrendered to the pistoleros and scofflaws. No doubt the town — or at least the author of the newspaper account — had breathed a big sigh of relief when Hickok packed up and left.

The mention of Wild Bill's retiring to his room for a nap, in light of my long hours reading in dim light, prompted me to do the same. I stumped my way upstairs to my room, unstrapped my leg and slid it under the bed, and massaged the stump as the sweat dried. I don't know if I snored as Wild Bill was reported to have done, but I certainly dozed off.

It was late afternoon when I stirred. Whether noise from the street or a stomach complaining about its emptiness awakened me I cannot say. Lacking the ability to stifle the clamor outside, I determined to do something about the rumbling within. Having breathed enough of Dyer's air for one day, I set out down the street in search of fresh air and a likely looking eatery.

A café whose window placards offered Chinese and American dishes proved the beginning and end of my pursuit. Bells hanging on the door announced my arrival, drawing the attention of a waiter in the Asian smock that reminds one of a night-shirt, a bao on his head, and a queue hanging down his back. Also noting my arrival were the only other patrons — seven cow-boys circled around a table, actually two tables, dragged together. They looked to have finished eating and were wreathed in smoke from foul-smelling cheap cigars, and passing around whiskey bottles far from full.

As I worked at emptying a plate of pork, rice, and chop suey washed down with tea, the cowboys laughed and joked. Given their jovial mood, I assumed the bottles they passed around weren't the first they'd enjoyed that day. I gathered from their conversation they'd ridden in from a ranch at some place called Horse Creek, trailing a small herd of steers for eastbound shipment, with more than the required number volunteering for the task so as to enjoy a night on the town.

The cowboys' conversation, as cowboy conversations are wont to do, turned to boasting and teasing about who was and was not a "top hand." A man claimed to be the best among them with a rope, only to be reminded about the time he went after a yearling heifer that escaped last spring's branding and, throwing his rope at the skittish heifer's heels fourteen times, missed every shot. Another alleged superior skill at "cuttin' critters from the bunch," yet another said he couldn't be beat when it came to throwing a "houlihan" loop to snare horses, and so on, every claim followed by good-natured joshing about a wreck or failure that belied the boast.

Things got really interesting when talk turned to "topping out broncs," with three of the cowboys claiming superiority. One, in particular, steered the conversation in a new direction. A black cowboy they called "Sam" said, "Aw, hell, boys, any one of you-all — and me — can ride the hurricane deck. That ain't nothin'."

"Oh? And just what is 'something' to your way of thinking, Sam?"

"Like I said, ridin' a cayuse is easy. I ain't never yet found one could throw me. A real hand, any man what lays claim to the title, he ought to could handle any kind of critter. Myself, I been aboard mules and mooses and elks and buffaloes and bears and what all. Ain't a one of 'em ever treated me to a mouthful of dirt. Plain fact is, boys, I can ride anything with hair on it!"

The outlandish claim roused a round of laughter and a rash of challenges from the crew. "Ah, hell, Sam," one said, "you ain't no kind of cowboy. I doubt you could fork that brindle milk cow in the barn back at the ranch."

Sam only laughed and allowed that bovine-type animals offered no challenge whatsoever.

"How's about that brockle-faced longhorn steer we brung in with the herd? You know, that bunch quitter we all took turns turnin' back into the herd all the way here? Think you could ride that ringy s-o-b?"

Sam laughed again. "If you-all can get 'im saddled, I can get 'im rode."

The steer in question was penned with the herd down at Cheyenne's so-called Elephant Corral, an outsize enclosure for holding cattle waiting to be loaded on rail cars. Rather than stage the contest there, the cowboys allowed as how they would bring the big steer into town and stage the event on the street.

One said, "Hell, yes! You remember when them cowboys from the Flyin' X had that buckin' horse contest on Sixteenth Street? Ol' Sam on that ringy steer's sure to stir up more excitement than that did! Boys, we might even make the newspapers!"

The cowboys left, laughing and backslapping and congratulating themselves on their pending extravaganza. I finished my supper and my tea and legged it over to Sixteenth Street to secure a suitable vantage point for the steer riding. Soon enough the cowboys arrived, a pair of them having ropes around the big steer's horns to drag him along, the rest of them riding alongside or behind the animal to keep him moving in the desired direction.

Once they reached the busiest part of the business district — which wasn't all that busy given the lateness of the afternoon, one of the cowboys roped the hind legs of the steer and stretched him out till he toppled over. Meanwhile, Sam had tied his horse to a hitching rail and pulled off the saddle. With much snorting and straining from both the bovine and the cowboys, the men managed to get the saddle cinched around the steer's belly and more or less centered on his back. They loosened their ropes and jumped aside. As the angry animal hoisted itself up on its hind legs in rising, Sam jumped into the saddle and found the stirrups.

"Ride 'im, Sam!"

"Hang on!"

"Put the spurs to 'im!"

"Watch him!"

The people on the street fled for safety as the cowboys cheered their saddle pal on, and the ruckus drew others from adjoining streets and out of the buildings.

A "ring-tailed fit" would not begin to describe the jumps and gyrations and bellowing of the steer. Sam hung on for dear life, even when the motion of the animal knocked him off kilter. The steer jumped onto the boardwalk and bucked his way along until in front of a clothing store with a plate glass window.

The steer tossed his head and saw his own reflection in the glass. He must have believed himself challenged by another steer, for he turned toward the window, lowered his head, and charged. The steer shattered the glass as he leapt through the window and into the store, which likely panicked the already wild and angry animal. We heard crashing and smashing as the steer rent a path of destruction through the store, the sound fading then intensifying as it turned back toward the missing window. Within seconds, it jumped back out, taking with it any remnants of glass still in the frame.

Still in the saddle despite the detour, Sam bellowed right along with his mount, laughing all the while. He loosed one hand from the saddle horn to pull away what appeared to be a pair of ladies underdrawers from his face. A flowered dress, pair of trousers, a shirt, and other assorted items of apparel flapped from the steer's horns and the saddle; a wrap of some kind flowed from Sam's waist like a sash.

The steer stumbled off the boardwalk and fell to its knees, breath heaving from flared nostrils. Sam declared victory and stepped out of the saddle, giving the steer a half-hearted kick in the ribs before walking away to raucous applause and well-wishes from the amused crowd. I doubted the owner of the clothing store would be amused when discovering the wreckage in his place of business.

Two of the mounted cowboys tossed loops around the animal's horns, a cowboy afoot grabbed the steer by the tail and hoisted it with a twist and the laughing cowboys led the spent — and considerably more docile than before — steer down the street to, I assume, rejoin the herd in the Elephant Corral.

Later that evening, the city marshal, in company with the proprietor of the clothing store, buttonholed the still-celebrating cowboys at the bar in McDaniel's, seeking payment for damages.

"What the hell you talkin' about, lawman? We was only just tryin' to subdue a steer on the prod!"

"If it wasn't for us, that ornery critter coulda hurt someone serious-like!"

"Darn right! We ought to be congratulated for our heroics!"

The marshal could barely suppress a smile. The businessman was not amused. "What about my store? The place is a shambles! Half my goods destroyed! My window gone!"

One of the cowboys laughed and slapped Sam on the back. "Hell, mister, you should be thankin' ol' Sam, here. If he hadn't of rode that ol' steer out of there, that critter would've really wrecked the place! Ask me, you oughta offer ol' Sam a reward!"

The storekeeper stuttered and stammered and remonstrated the cowboys, but they ignored him after a minute and turned back to their celebrating. The marshal let the citizen fume for a while, then advised him there would be no damages collected, owing to the cowboys' explanation and the absence of any witnesses to the contrary — or, at least, their refusal to contradict the cowboy version.

As for me, I sat at a table nursing a beer and watching the encounter. While I felt for the businessman and his losses, he was certainly more able to stand the expense than were the cowboys. Besides, the celebrating cowpunchers had provided an enjoyable early evening's entertainment, especially when stacked against the bloodshed I had witnessed in Abilene at the hands of drunken cowboys. By comparison, Sam and his compadres were relatively harmless.

After sending the clothing store owner away, the law officer suggested in no uncertain terms that the cowboys quit town before he changed his mind about locking them up for being drunk and disorderly. He suggested he might alter his opinion about collecting damages for their ill-advised rodeo in the streets of the city if they caused any more trouble.

The cowboys each raised a hand to the square, and with a smile swore the rising sun would find them long gone from the city of Cheyenne.

They were still at McDaniel's celebrating their adventure when I crossed the street to my room at Dyer's Hotel, where a soft bed awaited.

CHAPTER TWENTY-FOUR

Another undisturbed night's sleep found me lazing away in bed until awakened by the bright light of a sun nearing its zenith. I dressed and made my way to the lobby to stow my key and take advantage of the free lunch at the Senate Saloon, or perhaps across the street at McDaniel's.

"Good morning, Mister Collins."

"Likewise, Mister Zane."

"Please, call me Will."

"Certainly, Will. But only if you'll call me Pinebox."

With a smile, the clerk said he would be pleased to, but hotel policy forbade such familiarity.

"Fine, Will. I wouldn't want you to run afoul of your employer. But should you slip and let 'Pinebox' pass your lips, I will neither object nor report your transgression."

"Thank you, Pinebox," Zane — Will —

whispered, looking about with mock concern. Then, "Were you witness to the fiasco on Sixteenth Street last evening?"

"Indeed, I was. Quite the show."

"Those cowboys — they do get up to no good when they come to town."

"That is true. But, in this case, the boys were out for fun. Much preferable to violence, in my opinion."

Will sighed that sigh of his that often punctuated his conversation. "You're right, of course. There is much too much bloodshed in Cheyenne. Although it has lessened some since Charley Utter came through."

"You've mentioned that before — tell me about it, if you don't mind."

Will Zane cleared his throat and placed both hands on the registration desk. "Are you familiar with 'Colorado' Charley Utter?"

"No, I'm not. If I've heard his name in my travels, it did not register."

"Strange little man. Dresses like a dandy, always powdered and perfumed. They say he bathes daily — daily! That said, he lives the outdoor life. Trapper, prospector, trail guide. But, to answer your question, it seems Mister Utter, like so many, was afflicted with the latest contagion of gold fever and set out for the Black Hills from Denver.

"But he did not travel alone. Rather, he and his brother assembled a train of some thirty gaudy wagons occupied by a goodly share of Denver's demimonde, accompanied by gamblers and other undesirables. After a layover here in Cheyenne, they set out again taking with them — thank goodness — more of the same from here in the city.

"I will say this for Colorado Charley — he rid us of 'Madam Mustache' and 'Dirty Emma' and the soiled doves in their employ. And, as I mentioned before, your friend Wild Bill. Cheyenne should be ever grateful. The days and nights have been much more peaceful these past weeks since the wagon train departed."

"An interesting story, Will. Hold my key, if you please. I believe I'll find myself an early lunch."

"Try the lunch counter at the Senate. Much preferable to the offerings elsewhere, if I may offer an opinion."

I thanked Will Zane and was soon seated in a relatively quiet corner at the Senate with a plate of cold cuts and sliced bread and a foamy mug of tepid lager. The place was abuzz with drinkers and gamblers, never mind the early hour.

"Hey, you," came a voice from a few tables away. "You there, with the peg leg! Don't I know you?" The man who spoke slid back his chair and stood. It was Jim Levy, the gunfighter who fled Pioche after shooting and beating a man to death. He walked toward my table. "Ain't you that one-legged undertaker from Pioche? The one they call Pinebox?"

I nodded, uncertain of his purpose.

"Got yourself a new leg, didn't you? Had one looked like a snake, before."

Again, I nodded.

"Leave the man alone," a man I did not know said from his place at the bar.

Levy turned his attention to my defender.

"Shut the hell up, Charlie Harrison. This ain't nothin' to do with you. I'm just talkin' to an old friend."

"He a friend of yours?" the man called Charlie Harrison said to me.

"Not so you'd notice. I knew him — knew *of* him, saw him — in Pioche a while back."

"You heard him, Levy. He ain't no friend of yours. Now, leave him alone."

"Like I said, Harrison, it ain't none of your affair."

Harrison stood away from the bar and rested the heel of his hand atop the butt of a pistol holstered on his gun belt. He said he didn't like Irish and he didn't like Jews, and that was reason enough to kill Levy, what with him being both.

The argument stilled with the sound of the bartender slamming shut a double-barreled, breech-loading, sawed-off shotgun, followed by the clicking of the hammers pulled back by his thumb. He said nothing, simply eyed the contrarians and waved them toward the door with the barrels of his scattergun. Levy and Harrison watched each other without blinking as they sidestepped toward the door, Harrison arriving first and backing though the batwings. He stepped backward off the boardwalk, never taking his eyes off Levy as he came out the door.

"You'll take back what you said, Charlie, or I will shoot you down where you stand."

"Like hell I will."

I watched out a front window of the saloon as Levy sidled along the boardwalk, Harrison matching his steps along the street. Levy stepped off the sidewalk, landing between two horses tied at a hitchrail, pulling his pistol as he landed. Harrison drew his gun as well, and fired a shot at his partially hidden opponent, his bullet going high and into the wall of the saloon. Levy was buffeted about by the spooked horses, which caused Harrison's second shot to miss.

One of the horses, now sideways, all but completely concealed Levy, only his head showing above the animal. The horse shied and shuffled, but stilled long enough for Levy to rest his gun arm across the seat of the saddle and fire a shot that landed where Harrison's throat and chest met. The horse jumped again, then stood, and Levy's next slug blew a bloody hole in Harrison's chest. I had laid out enough bullet-riddled bodies over the years to know the lead had likely torn the man's heart to pieces.

I backed away from the window and dropped onto the first chair I bumped into.

The bartender, with a towel over his shoulder and still holding the shotgun, turned from the window where he had been standing beside me. "You don't look so good."

I swallowed hard. "I can't believe it. That man — that Harrison — he's dead. Dead, just for coming to my defense."

"Oh, I wouldn't worry about it, was I you. You were just an excuse."

"What do you mean?"

"Them two's been at each other for weeks. Near came to gunplay a time or two here in the Senate. Heard the same about them pickin' at each other in McDaniel's and down at Frenchy's, too. Probably every other saloon in town, I'll bet. It was bound to happen sooner or later."

"Still . . ."

"Like I said, fella, it weren't your fault. Don't worry about it."

I looked across the room at the beer I had barely touched, still showing a head of foam, and the plate of food next to it. My stomach turned at the sight. And so I left the Senate as fast as one good leg and one made of wood could carry me. Outside, Levy sat on the edge of the boardwalk in handcuffs. He looked at me, but I got the impression he did not see me.

But he did.

The marshal stood across the street, talking to a group of people I assumed witnessed the shooting. "Hey, law dog!" Levy hollered. "Here's who you oughta be talkin' to. Pinebox Collins, here — he saw the whole thing. Hell, he as good as started it."

Raising a hand to signal the witnesses he would be back, the marshal crossed the street, stepping around Harrison's body. "That true, mister?"

I shook my head, then thought better of it. "I saw it. All of it. But, no, I didn't start it."

"What's Levy talking about, then?"

With thumbs hooked into the armholes of

his vest, the marshal listened without interruption as I told how Levy recognized me and tried to start up a conversation. And how Charlie Harrison intervened, telling Levy to leave me alone, and the argument that followed. I recounted my recollection of the gunfight. Then, I suppose in an effort to cast aside any thought of my involvement, told the officer of the bartender's claim of an ongoing conflict between the two men.

"That's true enough. Levy and Harrison have been threatening to kill each other every time they cross paths. So it ain't like it's a surprise."

"Are you going to lock up Levy?"

"Oh, yeah. He'll spend the night in the jail. But I'll likely have to cut him loose come morning. Everyone I've talked to says it was a fair fight. I'll talk to the barkeep and anyone else in the Senate who's got something to say. But I don't suppose it'll change anything. I wish to hell I could lock up Levy and his like and lose the keys, but that ain't how things happen. Levy claims he knows you — that true?"

"Yes, in a way. Not like we knew each other, though. We were both in Pioche at the same time and that's as far as it goes. I suspect he was working for one of the mine owners. They all had gunmen on the payroll.

Most of them nothing but cold-blooded killers. Levy left town in a hurry after he beat a man to death when a bullet didn't kill him."

The marshal bid me good day, hoisted Levy off the sidewalk by the collar, and shoved him in the direction of the jail. The curiosity seekers had left by then and gone about their business as if there weren't a dead body lying in the street. In Cheyenne, in Pioche, in Abilene, it seemed people were as accustomed to violent death as soldiers on battlefields in the war. I was standing over Harrison when Russel Pomeroy drove up in a wagon.

"A good day to you, Mister Pinebox Collins. You didn't shoot this chap, did you?"

The question jolted me out of my reverie. "I'm sorry — what did you say?"

He smiled as he stepped down off the wagon seat and offered his hand. "Just wondering if you had taken up gunplay to stir up some undertaking business in the town," he said, chuckling and clapping me on the shoulder.

"No. I don't think you need my help for that."

"You think?" Pomeroy chuckled. "This is the first stiff I've seen since Colorado Charley came through here and lured away most every lowlife in town. Promised them a bonanza up in Deadwood, fleecing the miners that's been flocking in there like so many sheep." He stopped to shake out a handkerchief and blow his nose. "Hell, Pinebox, was I a young man like yourself, I might pull my picket pin and set out for the Black Hills myself."

I thought about what he said. Even though I still had plenty of money to keep body and soul together for the foreseeable future, sooner or later I would have to find work of some kind. The thought of heading east for more settled regions did not appeal. Putting down roots in the stony ground of Cheyenne did not seem feasible. But the thought of another rough-and-tumble town like Abilene had been, and Pioche still was, and Deadwood was certain to be, was likewise unsatisfactory. I was, I realized, at loose ends with no way to take up the slack.

"I don't know, Mister Pomeroy. I have to do something. All this sitting around reading old newspapers and drinking warm beer I've let go flat is wearing on me."

"Like I said, son, there's Deadwood. Ain't but two hundred, maybe two-fifty miles up the road. Climb on that Deadwood Stage and you could be there in no time. I suspect an undertaker could stay plenty busy up there."

"You're probably right. I just don't know if I want to go back to laying out shot-up gunfighters and crushed miners, trying to dodge all the holes in them to get them embalmed."

"Well, you could always go to Cincinnati or Philadelphia or someplace like that and hire on with some fancy funeral parlor and drain old ladies."

I allowed as how that sounded even less agreeable.

He said I could put my woodworking tools to use to build high-price coffins. "You'll never do that out West — maybe in some of the bigger cities, but even there folks tend to have simpler tastes and are less likely to shell out cash for frills that's going nowhere but into the ground."

For a minute or two I stared into nowhere thinking about what he said.

"C'mon, Pinebox. Help me get this body loaded and off the street before he sprouts."

I offered to help unload Harrison as well, and along the way to Pomeroy's place we talked more about prospects in Deadwood.

"Don't know how many embalmers there are up there already. But the place will keep growing as long as the gold holds out. Man could put together a pretty packet by then if he's smart. Spend the rest of his days down south in the sunshine, fishin' in the Gila River or anywhere else that suits him."

By the time we had Charlie Harrison laid out on the table and his clothing cut loose, Pomeroy had me convinced. I hobbled back to Dyer's Hotel. My appetite returned during the journey and I took what I believed would be my last meal in the Tin Restaurant. Sated, I stopped at the hotel desk to retrieve my key.

Will Zane was on duty. "Enjoy your meal, Mister Collins? — 'Pinebox,' as you prefer," he said with a wink as he fetched my key from its slot.

"Indeed, I did, Will. I will miss the wholesome food there you so heartily recommend."

Zane's eyes widened. "Will you be leaving us, Pinebox?"

"Yes. I believe I'll try my luck in Deadwood."

His eyes widened further. "Why, Mister Collins! Deadwood? There has been a veritable stampede through here for that destination for months. And not the type of people one would prefer! You'll remember Charley Utter's assemblage of reprobates I mentioned. The Black Hills are teeming with such! It is a *most* undesirable place! From what I hear, Deadwood is aptly named — going there is a death sentence for many."

I smiled. "You forget that I am an undertaker, Will. Death is my trade."

Zane's eye's widened yet again. He slapped my key onto the desk, turned away, and busied himself tidying a stack of receipts and other papers that did not need tidying.

CHAPTER TWENTY-FIVE

The Cheyenne and Black Hills Stage rolled into Fort Laramie, the jingle of harness chains and dust stirred by clomping hooves and spinning wheels filling the air. Packed into the Concord coach like cordwood, we spilled out the open doors for the brief layover there — for new teams and to distribute mail and express freight and grab a bite. I doffed my hat and swatted the dust off the other arm: the one that spent miles and hours hanging out the window.

Even as I did so, I reminded myself of the good fortune of most of my body being inside the Deadwood Stage rather than riding with the wind-torn and dust-buffeted riders up top, sandwiched among bags and baggage. Those men, despite the discomfort, counted themselves lucky to make the trip on the stagecoach in some three days, rather than spending the best part of a month as "passengers" on the hundreds of freight wagons on the way to Deadwood.

Mark Twain wrote profusely about stage-coach travel in his latest book, *Roughing It,* a copy of which I was well into and would appreciate having to hand to relieve the monotony. But the crowded conditions in the coach did not allow the luxury, the space being so confining you could not turn pages without jostling other riders, or comfortably read such a hefty tome with one hand hanging out the window.

Arching my back and rolling my shoulders cracked and popped some of the stiffness away and I hobbled my way into the stage station to see what was on offer in the way of food. I thought it likely, however, that a cup of filmy water and one of viscous coffee might be the only thing that would make it down my throat, given the revolting fare at most stage stations in my experience. As it happened, even the coffee wouldn't swallow, so I made my way outside to seek relief in the backhouse and stretch my leg until departure time.

As I reached out to swing open the out-house door, a buckskin-clad ruffian elbowed me aside, stepped inside, and slammed the door in my face. A few minutes later, the door banged open and again I was nearly knocked off my stump when the interloper exited. I finished my business and made my way to the coach. There he stood, checking the loads in his revolvers and thumbing cartridges into a short-barreled scattergun.

"Sorry to shove you out of the way back there, pard. But I was in something of a hurry to get here in time to ready my arsenal. Besides, even out here in the West it's ladies first."

My surprise must have been apparent, for our new shotgun guard smiled and extended a hand. "Martha Jane Canary. Some calls me Calamity Jane. I'll be ridin' shotgun on this here coach on into Deadwood."

"A pleasure, Miss Canary. I assure you there are no hard feelings." I handed her one of my cards, which she tucked into the top of her boot without giving it a look. "My name is Jonathon Collins. Like you, I am sometimes called by another name — 'Pinebox' in my case — as I am often an undertaker by trade."

"Plannin' to sell your wares in the Black Hills, are you? Not a bad idea, you ask me. There ain't no shortage of carcasses up there from what I hear. Likely to be more, too."

I asked if she had been to Deadwood.

"Nah. Ain't been yet. Closest I ever been was Rapid City, some time back. But just of late I was on my way to Deadwood Gulch with Colorado Charley's wagon train. Got stuck here and they went on 'thout me. Some'll tell you I got liquored up and locked in the hoosegow for drunk and disorderly, but don't you believe a word of it. Been sick is all. Anyways, I hired on to ride shotgun the rest of this trip. Been so many of these coaches robbed or attacked by Indians that the other guard, he didn't mind headin' on back to Cheyenne. Me, I got to get to Deadwood and hook up with ol' Wild Bill."

"Wild Bill? You know Wild Bill Hickok?"

She laughed. "Know 'im? Why sure I know 'im. Hell's afire, he's my intended!"

The coach squeaked as it rocked on the thoroughbraces when the driver climbed aboard. "C'mon, Jane. Get the folks on board and get on up here. This outfit's got schedules to keep, y'know."

"Keep your britches hitched, Johnny Slaughter. If you're a-waitin' on me, you're a-wastin' your time."

The second-class passengers clambered to the top of the coach and Martha Jane opened the door and shooed the first-class passengers inside. No one of the travelers had booked fare only as far as Fort Laramie, leaving us as crowded as before. I did hang back to board last, again taking the end of the middle bench, which lacked the comfort of a seat back but allowed the luxury of fresh air — and dust — through the window. Once my backside hit the seat, Martha Jane brought the door to, and after a couple of solid shoves to shift my bulk and that of the passengers beside me, managed to get it latched. Within seconds, "Calamity Jane" was on her seat, shotgun in hand. The driver released the brake and with his shouted obscenity and crack of the whip, the teams lunged into their collars, the tugs snapped taut, and the wheels on the Concord coach skidded and then rolled on toward Deadwood.

Somewhere beyond the verge of the Black Hills, but well shy of Custer City, I was thrown forward and out of my somnolence when the driver up top reeled in the lines, hollered "whoa!" and stomped on the brake. A glance out the window showed the wall of a defile just feet away. Jane leaned over the side. "Stay put, all of you. Road agents on horseback is blockin' our way. Don't do nothin' stupid."

Over the racket of the shuffling, snorting teams and clatter of the harnesses and hitches, I could hear a muffled voice but could not make out the words. The driver answered, whatever the question, with "Like hell I will. Now get out of my way."

The other voice again, louder this time but still indistinct.

Then, Slaughter. "You heard me the first time. Give us the road."

The next — and last — sound Johnny Slaughter made followed the crack of a pistol. It was an exhalation, almost a cough, followed by a groan. In short order, Martha Jane put the fire to both barrels of her scattergun. The coach lurched forward as the teams bolted, startled by the gunfire. I heard a clunk as Martha Jane dropped her shotgun at her feet. Horses screamed and hooves pounded and men cussed as the six horses and the Concord coach plowed a furrow through the midst of the bandits, knocking them aside and some, perhaps, down.

The coach never slowed on the ride into Custer City. From time to time I could hear the slap of the lines on the horses' backs as our shotgun-guard-turned-driver urged them on with shouts and whistles. Calamity Jane was standing in the seat, lines in hand when I unlatched the door and all but fell out of the coach when it rolled to a stop in town. Slumped over next to Jane, still in the driver's seat, was Johnny Slaughter. The windblown riders atop the coach barely

283

moved, their faces uniformly pale and drawn. Hostlers from the stage office attempted to calm the snorting, gasping, lathered horses as they unhitched them.

"Who the hell are you?" the station agent said, craning upward to face the woman on the seat. "What happened to Johnny?"

Calamity Jane turned loose the lines as the hostlers led the horses away, sat and picked up the shotgun, cracked open the breech and pulled out the spent cartridges. She tossed them to the ground at the agent's feet and reloaded both barrels from her coat pocket. "I be Martha Jane Canary. Johnny Slaughter, he be dead. Shot by bandits. I stood 'em off and brung in the stage. Saved your precious express box and all. Ain't the first time ol' Calamity Jane's been whip on a coach and likely won't be the last."

The agent looked on as two of the topside riders lowered Slaughter's body to men below. "Best come in and make a report."

Martha Jane snorted. "I done made my report. You heard it; you write it down. These passengers'll back me up." She dropped down and slapped me on the shoulder. "C'mon Pinebox. I'll stand you to a beer if that fancied-up tree stump of yours'll get you to the Pick & Shovel Saloon over yonder."

We carried our beers to an empty card table. Most of Custer City looked empty, most of its transient and former residents having decamped for Deadwood Gulch and the diggings there. Calamity asked about my lost leg and I recited the war story I had told so often I could do it in my sleep. She asked about the decorative peg leg and I told her I'd had occasion to turn wood while working in a cabinet shop, and made the peg leg on a whim.

"Wild Bill, he told me he knowed a feller one time had a wood leg what looked like it come off the front end of a Texas steer."

The swallow of beer in my throat stuck there, fighting against what wanted to be a cough from the other direction. The swallow won out and I cleared my throat. "He told you that?"

"Why, sure. Didn't I say so?"

I sipped a bit of beer. "That was me."

"The hell you say! You know my Bill?"

"Knew him some in Abilene. Saw him again in Kansas City. At the fair. That's where he saw my steer shank. I did not know it made such an impression on him."

"Oh, it did, all right. Ol' Wild Bill, he got a grin out of it, so he said. He takes a likin' to curious things, Bill does. Reckon that's why he took a shine to me. I ain't your normal kind of woman, as you seen."

She finished her beer before mine was half-gone and I fetched her another from the bar, there being no serving girls on duty. Martha Jane took a third of the beer in the mug in one long gulp.

"I don't mean to pry, Miss Canary —"

"Call me Martha Jane. Or Calamity, if it pleases you."

"Right. If you don't mind telling me, how did you come to be so, so . . . so 'not normal,' I guess I want to say."

"Oh, don't you worry none about upsettin' me, Pinebox. I been asked more questions and told more lies in reply than I can remember. But I'll tell it to you straight, you bein' a friend of Wild Bill, and all."

Martha Jane Canary told me she'd been born in Missouri, daughter of a gambler and sometime-prostitute, and had been given charge of three younger sisters and two younger brothers when she was but fourteen years old after her mother died in Montana.

"We never stayed long in Montana 'fore Pa took a notion to go to Utah Territory and take up farmin', which he did. But then he went and died on us no more'n a year later. Not bein' too partial to the Mormons, and them not bein' too partial to us, I sold out and loaded up the six of us in a wagon and went to Fort Bridger.

"We moved here 'n' there in Wyoming Territory, me doin' whatever I could put my hand to to keep food on the table for the young'ns. I worked in eatin' houses — cookin' and waitin' tables and washin' dishes. Drove ox teams for a freight outfit for a time. Was a dance-hall girl in a saloon. And I ain't proud to say it, but I spent time on my back at a hog ranch outside of Fort Laramie. Hell, Pinebox, I even did some scoutin' for the army out of Fort Russell. That's when I come to be called 'Calamity,' when I was a-workin' for the army."

Some, she told me, claimed the nickname came because those who insulted her were "courting calamity." But she denied that, claiming to be a mild-mannered and long-suffering sort, not given to easy offense. Rather, the moniker was bestowed by an army captain named Egan. She said she was on patrol with the troops, in pursuit of some recalcitrant Indians. The patrol had been ambushed and lost six of their number in the fighting. On the way back to the fort, they came under attack once again and the officer was wounded.

"I saw Captain Egan was hurt bad; his

horse was a-reelin' and Cap was about to lose his seat. Had he fell, them Indians would've had his hair. Spurrin' up my horse, I hurried back to where he was and rassled him off his horse and got him a-straddle of mine, him in the saddle and me behind, keepin' him from pitchin' off one side or t'other.

"We made it back to the post and when Cap got his wits about him, he said, 'I name you Calamity Jane, heroine of the plains.' On account of me rescuin' him from calamity, you see. And that's the truth of it."

Another beer bought me the story of her relationship with Wild Bill. She claimed to have been with him off and on at various places around the West, and that they had been lovers from time to time. "But there ain't no truth to the rumors that we got hitched and even had a baby. I ain't never had no babies, but if'n I was to, I can't think of no one I'd rather have father them than Wild Bill."

Her love for the man, she said, was now more protective in nature, and she had agreed to marry him for that reason. "Bill, he ain't as young as he once was. Hell, ain't nobody who is. But the years has been hard on Bill. He drinks too much, and it don't agree with him. His eyesight's a-failin', too.

'Bout all he can set his hand to nowadays is gambling, and that ain't exactly safe. Him bein' a famous gunfighter don't help none. You never know when some young whelp will call him out hopin' to cut a notch in his pistol grip and be known as the man that bested Wild Bill Hickok. He's stood 'em all off up till now, but, like I said, Bill ain't gettin' no younger and with his weak eyes and all . . . Well, his day's a-comin' and I aim to keep it from comin' any sooner'n what it has to. If I have any say in things, Wild Bill'll die in bed an old man."

Calamity Jane drained off the last of her beer and wiped her mouth with the sleeve of her buckskin coat, stained from performing the same task many times. "Well, hell, Pinebox. We ain't doin' no good a-settin' here makin' chin music. We best be a-gettin' on our way to Deadwood."

CHAPTER TWENTY-SIX

As soon as I stepped through the batwing doors in Nuttal & Mann's Saloon I saw Wild Bill Hickok at the far end of the bar. Back to the bar, he leaned against it with one boot heel hitched over the rail, whiskey glass in one hand and the other resting atop the butt of a revolver tucked into a red sash. His eyes were on me the moment I opened the door and followed as I walked toward him. As I drew closer he stood upright, set the glass on the bar, and turned to face me, his hand now drawing the revolver from the sash. My wooden leg clomped on the floor when I pulled up. Then I saw recognition fill Wild Bill's eyes.

"Well! It's Pinebox Collins, as I live and breathe. C'mon over, son, and wet your whistle. Sean, old boy," he said to the bartender, "draw my friend here a beer. On me." We shook hands and Bill clapped me on the shoulder. "Good to see you, son!"

Sean slid the foamy mug of beer down the polished bar — a novelty in Deadwood saloons, I would learn, most of which were cobbled-together outfits — and it slowed and stopped just shy of where Wild Bill stood. I stepped over to the bar and propped myself on an elbow.

"Son, if you don't mind, take a step away from me. I like to keep an eye on the door."

"You worried about something — or someone — Wild Bill?"

"Every time I draw a breath."

"Anything in particular?"

Wild Bill sipped his whiskey. "No. Not really. It just pays to keep your eyes open. You never know when somebody might decide to give ol' Wild Bill a try. Someone I bested at cards, maybe. Somebody bearin' a grudge. Kid with a gun tryin' to make a name for hisself. Hell, could be someone with no good reason at all."

I swirled my beer mug slowly in the wet sheen of condensation on the bar. "If you don't mind my asking, how are your eyes, Bill? I hear tell they are giving you trouble."

"Who told you that, son?"

I hesitated. "I've heard it here and there."

"I'd just as soon that kind of story didn't get around." He drank off the rest of his whiskey and signaled for another. "It'll only encourage them with ill intent to want to take me on." He sighed. "Sounds like it's too late to be worrying about it." A fresh drink arrived and he sampled it. "What you been up to, Pinebox? Kansas City seems like a hell of a long time ago."

Bill sipped his whiskey as I filled him in on my travels. Somewhere in the middle of my report on my time in Utah Territory, a chair scraped across the floor and crashed over backward and the noise in the room shut off as if someone had stuffed a cork in a bottle.

"You're cheatin' again, you sonofabitch!" the man standing over the tipped-over chair hollered, the bore of his pistol staring into the eyes of a card player across the table.

The man to the left of the angry loser said, "Sit down, mister. Nobody's cheating here. Better yet, find yourself a game somewhere else."

Wild Bill nudged me in the ribs and whispered, "That's Carl Mann — he owns the place, and he doesn't brook any non-sense."

The man with the gun turned it toward Mann. Mann's eyes shifted and he nodded so slightly the gunman didn't notice.

The accused cheater slammed a fist onto the tabletop. "Every time you lose a hand you think someone at the table is up to something," he said, picking up the deck and riffling the edges of the cards. "Simple fact is, you are not good at poker."

"Like hell. You-all are lined up ag'in me!" The barrel of the man's gun fanned back and forth at the other players, all wide-eyed and easing back, except Mann and the gambler accused of cheating, who appeared unconcerned.

Sean the bartender put an end to the standoff with a sharp rap of a truncheon. The gunman fell to his knees then toppled over. Two patrons answered Mann's request to haul the unconscious man outside.

"See what I mean, son? It pays to keep your eyes open," Wild Bill said. He signaled Sean for another whiskey. "Let's have a look-see at that peg leg of yours you say you made in Salt Lake City."

I hiked up my trouser leg and cocked my knee, raising the leg. Bill put down his drink, bent over with hands on knees and studied the rows of ridges and dips and Vs and valleys along the length of the limb.

"That's a right fancy bit of workmanship, I gotta say, Pinebox. But I admit bein' partial to the cow leg you was sportin' back in Kansas City."

I digressed in my story to recount the

demise of the steer stump in Pioche, and of its hand-carved replacement of a coiled snake carved from a cedar limb.

"I would purely love to see that snake, Pinebox. It still with you?"

"Yes. I keep it as a spare, should this one get damaged. But it is stowed in a trunk with my embalming equipment and wood-working tools and some books. As of now, it is on a freight wagon someone between here and Cheyenne. Much closer to Cheyenne than here, I fear."

"Well, when it shows up, strap it on and trot it out for me. It would be a sight to see, I'm sure."

Promising to do so, I asked Bill about what he had been up to. "I read something in the papers years back about you being in a show with Buffalo Bill Cody."

"Ah, son, that was a sad time for an old frontiersman. I was uneasy about the whole idea, but that damn Cody, he can talk a flea off a dog's back. It was troublesome, I'll tell you. I couldn't ever remember my lines — it all just got jumbled up in my mind every time I stepped onto a stage in front of all them folks. And that damn limelight they shine in your face fixes it so you can't see a blamed thing. I was glad to be shut of the whole deal. I just ain't cut out to be a performer."

Wild Bill said he kept busy with this and that after giving up acting, mostly earning his keep at the poker tables — a fickle and flighty way of living, he claimed, that shuffled from high to low by chance and luck. Other opportunities presented themselves from time to time. He said he first went to Cheyenne to guide and scout for a hunting expedition, then stayed for a time gambling, wandered back to Kansas City and St. Louis, and back again to Cheyenne.

"What you said about my eyes, Pinebox . . . well, it's true enough. Not that I want it getting around, you understand. First it was just that things would get blurry, and light hurt my eyes. Then my eyeballs would feel like they might pop out of my head. Saw some kind of fancy doc in Kansas City and he told me there wasn't nothin' to be done for it, and it will likely get worse. Could be I'll go blind altogether."

My beer crept lower in the mug, leaving a lacy residue of foam. Sean kept Wild Bill's shot glass filled, and he emptied it with the regularity of a chiming clock. As we talked, he kept an eye on the card tables as if waiting for a seat to empty in the right game.

"I hear tell you are getting married."

"Who told you that, son?"

"Lady I met on the way up here. Calamity Jane. She said the two of you were gettin' hitched."

Wild Bill chuckled. "Ol' Martha Jane, she's always tryin' to get her hooks into me. But she's too late. Got hitched already. Married sweet Agnes. Agnes Lake. Quite a woman, my Aggie. Met her back east some years back. Workin' for a circus, she was. Fancy horseback riding. And she could walk on them high wires. Next time I saw her, she was runnin' the show.

"Well, we met up in Cheyenne and decided to get married and live out our lives together right there in Cheyenne." Something struck him funny and he laughed aloud, gulped down a glass of whiskey, laughed again. "There was plenty of folks thought ol' Wild Bill wasn't a good prospect for a husband. Including that Methodist preacher we stood up in front of and did the deed. One of his flock told me he read in the marriage book there at the church where the record was wrote down that the sky pilot wrote about me, 'Don't think he meant it.' Fact is, I wasn't so sure myself, at first. But bein' with Aggie agrees with me."

"How is it you're here and she's back in Cheyenne?"

"That's but a temporary thing. I'll be gettin' back to her soon enough. Never meant to leave, but when Colorado Charley came through Cheyenne with that traveling troupe of his, singin' the praises of Deadwood, it sounded like a worthwhile adventure. When Charley cut me in for a piece of the action, Aggie gave me her blessing. Money's been good — Charley was right about that. I figure to parlay it into a good-size poke playin' cards with these shovel stiffs and double jackers, then head on back to Cheyenne and wedded bliss."

I resisted asking more about Calamity Jane. Two men stood up at one of the poker tables, one throwing his cards down in disgust.

"Sorry, Pinebox. It's time I got to work."

I swallowed the last of the beer in my mug, by now tepid and flat. The hour being late, I determined to make my way to Charley Utter's camp and my bedroll.

At the table, Hickok convinced one of the players — the one with his back to the wall — to move to another chair. Wild Bill took the vacated seat, squirmed his backside into a comfortable place, and pushed a stack of bank notes toward the dealer to buy his way into the game and purchase a pile of chips. Hickok was known to the other players but some were strangers to him, so the dealer offered introductions. I could not hear all the names, but remember two of the players in the game. One was introduced as Captain Bill Massie.

The other, Jack McCall.

Chapter Twenty-Seven

The whistling of a cheery tune awakened me from dreamless sleep. I crawled out of my bedroll and poked my head out of the shelter tent to see Colorado Charley coming into camp. The long curls hanging damp on his shoulders and his face with that just-shaved sheen said he was back from the bathhouse and his daily ablutions.

"Top of the morning to you, Pinebox," he said, then whistled out the last few doo-dah notes of "Camptown Races."

"Good morning, Mister Utter," I said around a stretch and a yawn. "How are things in town?"

"As usual. Busy and abuzz. Shift change at the mines, so plenty of folks about."

I scrubbed the sleep off my face with a brisk rub with the palms of my hands. "I've been thinking," I said with another yawn. "Prospects look good for an undertaking parlor. I haven't noticed there being one here — not that I've given the city a thorough look. Do you know of any?"

"Can't say as I do. There's a cemetery up the hill. Of course, you'd expect that. Who puts the bodies there I can't say. Must be somebody boxing them up."

"I believe I'll look into it today. Who would I see about getting a license for a business, or to locate a suitable site?"

Utter laughed. "Look in the mirror. You've got as much authority in Deadwood as anyone. Like I said, there's no government or regulations of any such niceties here."

Utter slipped through the flap of his big tent and I could hear him rustling around. He was back out within a minute or two, tying a red sash around his waist. That particular fashion item was popular around the West in those days. For some, like Wild Bill, the sash served a purpose, doubling as a gun belt. But for others, like Charley and other dandies, it was all for show. He slid the sleeves of a fresh starched shirt into his buckskin jacket. "Best of luck in your search, Pinebox. I'm off to town to look after my business interests. Could be we'll cross paths."

After breakfast at a likely looking hash house — a permanent-looking establishment in a wood-frame building, rather than canvas — I set out into the streets of Deadwood searching for a practitioner of The Dismal Trade. Not wanting to negotiate the up-and-down, potholed-and-rutted, dusty-and-muddy thoroughfares of Deadwood, I hired a riding mule at a livery stable. My stirrup pouch for my peg leg was somewhere in transit, so I had to be content — and somewhat uncomfortable — letting it dangle. Still, plodding through the streets muleback would prove less taxing than going afoot.

Of all the gaudy signs adorning Deadwood's businesses, whether homemade, slapdash affairs or those professionally rendered, none indicated any presence of a professional undertaker. Nor did the construction of coffins merit mention at any of the carpentry or cabinetry establishments I espied. Still, beyond the sign marking Ingleside Cemetery were several freshly filled graves, so there could be no doubt that someone, somewhere, was preparing bodies for burial.

I dismounted and sat in the shade of a pine tree to think, resting my back against the gnarly bark of its trunk. A jerk of the reins in my hand stirred me from half sleep. The mule's head was up, ears alert and pointing down the path leading to the

301

graveyard. Soon came the sound of a drum, beating out a funereal cadence. Then the procession came in sight, a thin man in a stovepipe hat and swallowtail coat leading the way, looking for all the world like a dime novel rendering of an undertaker. A rough coffin borne on the shoulders of six men followed, trailed by five mourners with the drummer bringing up the rear.

The parade passed around the side of the hill and stopped where there must have been a dug grave, concealed from my view across the low rise. The coffin disappeared from view as the pallbearers lowered it to the ground and I watched the men, visible from the waist up as they gathered round. No preacher was evident among them, but one man pulled a Bible or prayer book from where he'd slid it under the waist of his pants in the small of his back and read from its pages, none of the sound reaching me.

After a few minutes, the mourners put their hats on their heads and filed out of the bone garden and back toward the city. The undertaker and two of the mourners stayed behind and from their activity I knew they were lowering the coffin into the earth with ropes. The fancy-dressed man in the stovepipe hat looked on as the other two wielded shovels to fill the grave with the efficiency of practiced muckers.

When the trio came around the hill, I waited beside the path, reins in hand and the mule standing by. The weedy man in the stovepipe hat signaled his helpers on their way, watched them go, then turned to me.

"I sense you want a word, friend."

"I do, if you've a moment." He did not reply. "I take it you are an undertaker."

The man smiled and tugged at the lapels of the long-tailed coat. "Only by circumstance. I am a doctor. Doctor Ellis Pierce. One of few in Deadwood. But even given the shortage, doctors are abundant when compared to undertakers, so I act in that capacity when called upon. Few of the residents of our fair city care for the niceties as most are men here without family or other relations. Most of our dead go into the ground without ceremony. But when a proper laying-out is wanted, I provide — even going so far as to embalm the deceased's body if desired."

Lifting his hat and mopping his brow with a frayed handkerchief, the doctor wondered at the reason for my curiosity. For some reason — perhaps his manner or attitude or appearance suggested caution — I did not want to tip my hand at the time, so used the excuse of an ailing friend not long for this world.

"Stop by my place this afternoon," Pierce said. "We can discuss arrangements in whatever depth you desire. I will, of course, be seeing patients but there should be no difficulty in finding time to visit. Bring your friend along if you wish. Perhaps, with proper medical care, his need for undertaking services will prove unnecessary — at least for the present."

He told me the location of his office and living quarters, touched a finger to the brim of his tall hat, and walked away.

The day was getting hot and the customary time for dinner had come and gone. I decided to return the ambling mule to the livery and tuck into a meal. Sensing he was on the way home where shade and sustenance might await, my mount stepped into a jogtrot and would not desist despite my nearly continuous tugging on the reins. Lacking the leverage of two feet in the stirrups feet to rise to the rhythm of the mule's gait, I bounced and rattled my way to the stable then slid out of the saddle, glad to have foot and peg on firm ground.

No sooner had I settled the bill than a wagon rattled into the yard with Calamity Jane on the seat. She hauled back on the lines and the team stopped, snorting and jingling bits and harnesses as they shook their heads and pawed the ground.

"Hey there, Pinebox! What're you up to?"

"Nothing of note, Jane. How about yourself?"

"Hired on to carry hay up to the Homestake. They lower it down the hole to feed them mules they got down there to haul the ore cars." She shook her head. "Hell of a life for a critter, you ask me — even a mule. Most of 'em won't never see daylight again."

"I am just fixing to find myself a meal, Jane. Care to join me?"

"Why, I'd be delighted." She stepped off the wagon and wrapped the lines around the brake handle. A whistle brought a hostler out of the depths of the stable to take charge of the team and wagon and Jane and I set out in pursuit of a meal. While I anticipated a hot meal, Jane declared an intolerable thirst and so it was the lunch counter at the Double Jack Saloon for me. Her fare consisted of wine for the main course and beer for dessert. I feasted from the free lunch counter on dry bread, dill pickles, pickled eggs, crumbly cheese, sliced roast beef I could have soled my boots with, and ham that would have been better yesterday.

Once Calamity Jane had cut the dust in her throat, she asked about my reunion with Wild Bill.

"How did you know about that?"

"Oh, I saw Bill myself, just this morning. I was up early to haul that hay and he was up late after gamblin' at Nuttal & Mann's. Didn't talk long. Asked if he'd seen you yet; he said he did." Jane gurgled down more wine. "Did all right with the cards, he said. Won a pretty good pile. Cleaned out some fella name of McCall who weren't none too pleased about it. Then Bill — bein' a generous sort — flipped him a half eagle 'cross the table and told him to get hisself some breakfast. Bill, he didn't see no hurt in it, but knowin' men like I do, I reckon he wounded the man's pride some."

Jane watched me eating the lunch counter food. "Don't know how you can eat that stuff, Pinebox. As likely to kill you as not."

I swallowed a wad of bread and beef. "Better than starving to death."

"Not by much."

"Or drinking yourself to death."

She shook her head. "I worry 'bout that with ol' Bill."

I laughed. "I was thinking of you, Calamity Jane."

"No need to worry 'bout me. My gut's

lined with cast iron. But Bill — well, if his ever was, it's rusted through by now." She sipped her wine, then said, "He seem all right to you?"

"He was drinking plenty. But he did the same back in Abilene, as I recall. The effects of alcohol don't seem to show on him much. He always appears to have his wits about him."

"I'll give him that."

"From what he said — and I trust you know this already, being his friend — he's worried more about his eyes. Says they cause him pain, and his vision is failing him."

"He does find it troublesome. Don't know as there's anything to be done for it, from what them big-city docs told him." Jane's forehead furrowed; she shook her head and took a long drink of wine. "That's why I intend to marry up with him — so's I can look out for him in his declinin' years."

I wiped up a spot of mustard from my plate with a bite of bread and chewed it, thinking it best not to broach Calamity Jane about the wife Bill already had. I pushed back from the table. "Best be on my way, Jane. There's a doctor I need to see."

" 'Bout Wild Bill?"

"No. Not that."

"You ailin'?"

"Oh no — just want to see this Doctor Pierce in relation to setting myself up in business here in Deadwood."

"Sounds 'bout as exciting as watchin' Bill Cody gut a buffalo."

I laughed, left Jane with her wine, and made my way through the streets to where Doctor Pierce said I would find him. He was there, but the patients he warned about were absent.

"Ah!" he said, looking up from his seat at a desk in his small outer office. "You were at Ingleside earlier. Interested in undertaking, as I recall."

I nodded, uncomfortable with the deception.

"Don't believe I caught your name."

"Collins. Jonathon Collins." I could not have said why suspicion lingered, but I did not offer him one of my cards the way I usually do when making an acquaintance. Something about the man just didn't seem right.

"What is it you would like to know, Mister Collins?"

"Just curious about how you go about your work, I guess."

"Well, come on back."

Pierce escorted me through a door into a

short hallway with a door at the opposite end and one on each side. His living quarters were to the left, he said. He opened the door on the right to reveal his examination room.

"Here's where I do my doctoring — when I can get a patient to come here, that is. Most times I am called out." He opened a glass-fronted cabinet and pulled out a bottle. "Do you know of this medicine? Morphine? It might be an overstatement to call it a medical miracle, but not by much. Its efficacy when injected to relieve pain of most any kind is remarkable. I use it to treat many maladies."

"I have heard of it, but that is all."

"Marvelous thing, morphine."

"I have heard people become dependent on it."

He nodded, then shook his head as he put the bottle back in the cabinet. "That is a risk. Some patients come to believe they cannot do without it. When I will no longer treat them, some wind up in the opium dens. It's sad, really. But that is not why you came to see me. Come this way."

The doctor showed me through the door at the end of the hallway into a sparsely furnished room. A shelf hanging from the wall held a few bottles of embalming chemicals, along with other bottles I did not recognize. The table for laying out bodies was nothing more than two blood-stained, rough-sawn planks nailed to crosspieces at each end, to which were nailed legs and their braces. The whole affair looked unstable — and uncomfortable, which really would not matter to those placed upon it, but, still, it seemed disrespectful.

A few coffins stood against the wall. At first glance they appeared to be run-of-the-mill six-board coffins. But a closer look revealed shoddy workmanship. The joints showed gaps, the boards were poorly fit, and the lining was nothing more than muslin tacked into place, showing rough and frayed edges.

Pierce stood by as I studied the room, hands clasped behind his back. "It isn't fancy. But this room serves its purpose."

"You said you did embalming. How does that work?"

Suppressing a smile, he stepped to the shelf. "I have no formal training but have read up on it and devised my own methods." He took a metal box from the shelf, placed it on the table, unlatched and lifted the lid. Inside was an oversize hypodermic syringe, some wide-bore needles, and a few lengths of tubing. "I use this to inject my own mixture of commercial embalming fluid and other chemicals into the circulatory system of the departed, displacing and replacing the lifeblood."

I nodded, fearing if I spoke I would regret my words. Pierce's tools, and the workmanship they implied, revealed a dearth of knowledge concerning the art of arterial embalming. There was not a chance in hell his methods could adequately preserve a body.

Two things were foremost in my thoughts: a hope that I would not fall ill in Deadwood and require medical treatment from this man, and impatience for the arrival of my undertaking apparatus so I could set up shop in the Black Hills and provide services of a kind both effective in their utility and respectful of the dead. Doctor Pierce's techniques were neither.

CHAPTER TWENTY-EIGHT

I found Wild Bill that evening much as I had the night before — back against the bar, heel hooked on the rail, drink in hand, surveying the crowd and studying everyone who entered Nuttal & Mann's Saloon.

"Buy you a drink, Bill?"

"Sure as you're born, Pinebox."

Hickok turned and set his glass on the bar, signaling Sean the bartender to refill it. On the way over, he stopped to draw me a mug of beer.

Taking half the whiskey in a gulp, Wild Bill belched and patted himself on the stomach. He asked what I'd been up to.

"Looking the city over. Trying to figure how to set up in business here."

"Planting corpses?"

I nodded. "That, and nailing up coffins. From what I've seen, there's a crying need for both services."

"I suspect you'll sort it out, Pinebox.

Young feller like you with most of his life in front of him . . ." He shook his head, swallowed the rest of his whiskey, and raised the glass in Sean's direction.

"Ah, Bill, you're not that old."

He chuckled. "Not in years, maybe. But I feel like an old horse that's been rode hard and put up wet too many times." Bill reached into a pocket with thumb and finger and drew out a folded-up sheet of writing paper. "Do me a favor, Pinebox. This here's a letter to Aggie. Post it for me, will you? Don't know when I'll get a chance to send it, sleepin' all day like I do."

"Sure. Be happy to."

He unfolded it and passed it to me. "Go on ahead. Read it."

"You sure you want me to?"

He nodded and I looked the letter over. It was brief, but his spidery scrawl took some time to decipher. *Agnes Darling,* he had written, *if such should be we never meet again, while firing my last shot, I will gently breathe the name of my wife — Agnes — and with wishes even for my enemies I will make the plunge and try to swim to the other shore.*

I did not know what to say, so I folded the letter carefully and slid it into a pocket.

"Bill!" The call came from Carl Mann, seated at one of the poker tables. Occupying another seat was the man I'd heard introduced the night before, the man they called Captain Massie. A player whose name I did not know, but whose name I later learned was Chuck Rich, sat with his back to the wall. The fourth man at the table was gathering what money he had left in disgust and, none too happy, left the game, done for the night.

Mann tapped the deck of cards against the table, tidying up the alignment of the edges. "Got an empty chair here, Bill — come on and sit. Give me a chance to win back some of what you've been takin' from me at these tables of mine."

"Don't mind if I do, Mann." Wild Bill carried his glass to the table. "How about you switch seats, Rich?"

The gambler eyed Wild Bill with wrinkled brow. "Why's that, Hickok?"

"I like to sit with my back to the wall when I play. Everybody knows that."

"Well, I don't know it and I don't care. I've had good luck sittin' right where I am and I guess I'll stay right here."

"I'm asking nice," Bill said.

"Don't care."

Carl Mann said, "C'mon Rich. What difference does it make?"

"Don't make no difference to me. It's

Hickok you ought to be talkin' to. Speakin' of talk — we gonna do that all night, or are we gonna play poker?"

All eyes were on Wild Bill. After a moment, he shrugged and took the empty chair opposite Rich and between Mann and Massie. They played a few hands with little enthusiasm, the betting as low as the hands dealt. Then came a round more to the liking of the gamblers, as they bet and raised around the table.

The bet came to Wild Bill. He picked up his hand, fanned the cards, and studied them. He studied the other players. Looked again at his cards. He reached for his stack of chips. Bill never placed the bet.

"Damn you, take that!" came a yell, punctuated with the report of a forty-five-caliber pistol in the hand of Jack McCall — the man whose money Wild Bill had taken at poker the night before — held inches from the back of Hickok's head.

As quickly as McCall had entered Nuttal & Mann's and stolen up behind Wild Bill, he ran back out the door. Smoke from the pistol hung heavy in the air as Wild Bill Hickok's head, ripped asunder by the bullet, rested on the poker table and spilled blood onto his poker hand — a pair of aces and a pair of eights, all black.

315

I do not recall number nor suit of the fifth and final card.

CHAPTER TWENTY-NINE

Jack McCall's bullet had burned a hole through Wild Bill Hickok's head, killing him dead as it went, then punched its way out through his right cheek and hit Captain Massie in the wrist. Massie's other hand grabbed the wound, covering it, but blood seeped out between his fingers. "Sonofabitch!" Massie said. "Wild Bill shot me!"

Then he noticed Hickok, sprawled on the table, blood streaming from his wound. "No! Oh no!" He stood, tipping over his chair, and backed away from the table. Rich's chair scraped across the floor as he slid back from the table.

"Somebody get after McCall," Mann said. "Don't let him get away. Sean, fetch Doc Pierce!"

It should go without saying that I am — and was that night — no stranger to death. But the shock of seeing a friend gunned down like that nailed me to the floor. I

317

struggled to catch my breath. Beer dribbled from the tipped mug in my shaking hand, splashing onto my boot and peg leg. When I came to myself and looked around, most men in the saloon seemed to be in similar straits. Only Carl Mann kept his wits about him, again encouraging the agog gamblers and drinkers in his establishment to get out and find McCall before he slipped away into the hills.

I made my way to the table and laid a finger on Wild Bill's wrist where it lay on the table among the scattered chips like his final contribution to the pot. Finding no trace of a heartbeat, I turned away and left Nuttal & Mann's Saloon for what I expected to be the last time.

"Charley!" I yelled as I brushed aside the flap over the entrance to his tent.

The ratcheting of the hammer on a cocking pistol pulled me up short. "Stop right there, mister, or you'll die where you stand!"

"It's me, Charley — Pinebox Collins."

"I don't care who you are. Get the hell out of my tent. Nobody comes into my tent."

"Wild Bill's been shot."

I heard Utter pull back the hammer and lower it to rest at half cock. "What are you saying?"

"Wild Bill's been shot. Up at Nuttal & Mann's. He's dead."

"Wait outside. Give me a minute to get dressed."

In next to no time, Colorado Charley Utter pushed out through the tent flaps. I could not see him well in the dim glow from the dying campfire but he looked for all the world as if he'd just stepped out of a clothier after a trip to a bathhouse.

He checked the loads in this revolver, tucked it into its holster, and snapped the lapels of his buckskin jacket. "I'll see to it," he said, and walked out of the firelight.

Seeing no reasonable alternative, I crawled into my shelter tent and collapsed on the bedroll, not bothering to undress or even remove my leg. The next thing I remembered was a tug on that peg leg, gently at first but then dragging me out from under the canvas.

"C'mon, Pinebox! Get up and piss, the world's on fire," Calamity Jane said.

I rolled over onto my back and elbowed my way upward to sit. With the palms of both hands, I scrubbed the smear of sleep off my face. I looked up to see Jane silhouetted against the dawn sky, arms akimbo.

She kicked me on the peg leg. "Let's go. We're a-burnin' daylight."

"Daylight? The sun isn't even up yet."

She kicked again. "Get up. We got to go help Colorado Charley tend to Wild Bill."

Wild Bill. I felt the blood rush from my face and my knees go weak as last night's murder of Wild Bill Hickok replayed in my head. "Damn," I said under my breath. I turned over and levered myself upright on my good leg. I brushed off the seat of my pants and tugged my clothing into some semblance of order. "Let's go."

I hobbled along as best I could in Calamity Jane's wake, hustling to keep up with the swish of her buckskin britches as she strode along. A meet-up with Colorado Charley must have already been arranged, for we made a beeline to an eating house on the main street of Deadwood. Utter was seated at a back table when we arrived.

"Jane. Pinebox," he said, rising to pull out a chair for Calamity.

He waved over the serving girl to pour us coffee and top off his half-filled cup. I sipped at mine, the brew too hot to swallow. Jane saucered her coffee, blowing across the puddle to cool it, slurping it over the edge, and pouring more onto the shallow saucer to cool.

"Tell us what happened, Pinebox," Charley said. "I heard it from some of the men who were there, but would like to hear it from you."

"Hard to say. It was over before I knew it was happening." I related the story with as much detail as I could remember, which wasn't much.

Jane snorted. "It was for sure that damn 'Broken Nose' McCall who shot 'im?"

I nodded.

"They caught him," Charley said.

"He's in jail?"

"Jail?" Charley laughed. "There is no jail in Deadwood, Pinebox. Like I told you, there is no semblance of law or government here. But McCall won't be going anywhere — he's chained to a tree."

"So, what happens now?"

"Oh, the town's leading citizens will convene a court of sorts. Miner's courts, they call them. Kangaroo court, more like it."

Jane said, "What about Bill? Where's he?"

"By the time I got up to Nuttal & Mann's, Doc Pierce was already there. He took Bill's body to his place. Said he'd get him embalmed and ready for burial. At my expense, of course."

My cup clattered as I dropped it onto the saucer, sloshing coffee onto the tabletop. "Pierce! The man's no undertaker! Pierce doesn't know the first thing about embalming. Hasn't even got the proper equipment."

Colorado Charley stared at me, his face blank. "What are you saying?"

"I'm saying there's no way we can let Pierce lay out Wild Bill. He'll botch the job as sure as I'm sitting here."

"What ought we to do?" Jane said.

I had no answer.

"Just as I thought," Utter said. "There's nothing we can do. Until you hang up your shingle, Pinebox, Pierce is what we've got."

Jane stood and said her goodbyes. "I'll pay a visit to that doctor. Tell him if he messes up with Wild Bill he'll have me to answer to."

Charley stood as she left, then sat down again. "I'll be at the newspaper office soon as it opens. I'll post a notice that we'll be holding a funeral for Bill at my camp." He emptied his coffee cup. "I'm awful sorry. But I don't see any alternative to Doc Pierce. All we can do is hope for the best."

Alone at the table, I read and reread Wild Bill's last letter to his wife in Cheyenne. She would have heard of her husband's demise by the time it arrived, but, still, I thought to write a short note of my own to send along with it, expressing my condolences and relating the manner of Bill's death, glossing over the most upsetting of the details. At the very least, "Aggie" deserved a firsthand account from one who was there at the end, as well as someone who cared for the man.

I don't really remember much of what I did after posting Wild Bill's letter. I know I spent most of the day at Charley's camp, perhaps intending to tidy up the place — a fool's errand, given Utter's fastidious ways. For some reason, the shooting of Wild Bill took it out of me, and I lacked the gumption to do much of anything but sit around camp and read. I was well into Mark Twain's *Roughing It,* but do not ask me to recall a single word from the many pages I supposedly read that day.

Colorado Charley awakened me the next morning after a night of fitful sleep, thrusting a copy of that morning's *Black Hills Pioneer* under my nose, pointer finger tapping his posted notice, so fresh the ink all but smeared at his touch.

Died in Deadwood, Black Hills, August 2, 1876, from the effects of a pistol shot, J. B. Hickok (Wild Bill) formerly of Cheyenne, Wyoming. Funeral services will be held at Charley Utter's Camp, on Thursday afternoon at 3 o'clock, P.M. All are respectfully invited to attend.

Few of Deadwood's residents knew Wild Bill Hickok. But everyone, without exception, knew who he was. The man had been a legend on the frontier for years, with a reputation that flourished more between the covers of dime novels than in real life. Still and all, James Butler Hickok was without doubt a man deserving of acclaim. I had personally witnessed his bravery and daring, and never had I detected even a hint of fear or cowardice. He was far from perfect, but who among us is not?

It was the man's reputation rather than personal acquaintance that attracted the crowd to Wild Bill's funeral service. It appeared most of the city, save those on shift at the mines, crowded into the clearing and spilled up and down the ridge into the trees. The open coffin stood propped against the trunk of a pine tree. The corpse looked presentable, I had to admit. There was little to be done with the bullet hole in Bill's cheek, but Pierce had cleaned it up as best he could. But you could not tell from the outside what Pierce and his slapdash embalming methods had done inside, if anything at all.

Colorado Charley eulogized his friend fervently, holding forth long beyond the patience of the assembled crowd. Charley oversaw the closing of the coffin and I joined five others Charley chose as pallbearers — only one of which, Carl Mann, I knew — in hefting the coffin to our shoulders. We carried it down to the road and slid it into the back of a wagon driven by Calamity Jane for transport to Deadwood's Ingleside Cemetery. Most of the city's citizens went their separate ways, but a goodly number paraded along behind. At the graveyard entrance we again took up our burden and carried what was left of Wild Bill to his place of eternal rest.

Or so we thought.

As we lowered the box into the ground and took our turn tossing in a handful of dirt, a preacher Charley recruited from where I do not know read from the Book of Common Prayer.

In sure and certain hope of the resurrection to eternal life through our Lord Jesus Christ, we commend to Almighty God our brother James Butler Hickok, and we commit his body to the ground; earth to earth, ashes to ashes, dust to dust. The Lord bless him and keep him, the Lord make his face to shine upon him and be gracious unto him, the Lord lift up his countenance upon him and give him peace. Amen.

I stayed behind to put more than a handful of dirt into the grave. Once it was filled, Colorado Charley fetched a tall wooden marker from the wagon to adorn the grave. How he managed to have such a lengthy tribute carved in so short a time I have no idea. We planted it at the head of the grave then stood back and read.

Wild Bill, J. B. Hickock killed by the assassin Jack McCall in Deadwood, Black Hills, August 2d, 1876. Pard, we will meet again in the happy hunting ground to part no more. Good bye, Colorado Charley, C. H. Utter.

Morning found me among the crowd at the Langrishe Theater for the so-called trial of the cowardly Jack McCall. There was, of course, no legality or authority to the affair, but frontier justice being what it was at many times and places in the West, the man appointed judge banged his gavel and called the affair to order.

Men were appointed to prosecute and defend McCall, and witnesses sworn. Under questioning of witnesses, those impaneled as jurors learned that after the shooting, McCall ran from the saloon and attempted to make his escape on a stolen horse, but upon tying the animal to the hitch rail, the owner had slackened the cinch, the result being McCall falling off into the street when the saddle slipped. And so he ran away afoot and attempted unsuccessfully to hide out in a butcher shop, where he was apprehended by several men from the saloon and the street.

"Jack does not deny shooting Wild Bill," the storekeeper appointed to represent the killer said. "But we say it was justifiable homicide."

"That sonofabitch Hickok killed my brother," McCall claimed. "Back in Abilene. He might've been a lawman when he did it, but it wasn't nothin' but cold-blooded murder. Left him to bleed out in an alley, backshot. I killed Hickok to revenge my brother's blood, and by damn I'd do it again."

The prosecutor held that Wild Bill had insulted McCall by giving him a coin to buy breakfast after taking his money at poker, and the killing was nothing more than cold-blooded revenge murder.

McCall held firm.

The prosecutor then contended the shooting was a matter of pernicious pride, and that McCall shot Hickok in order to gain a reputation as a fearsome gunman.

McCall held firm.

The show took less time than Wild Bill's funeral. The miners and shopkeepers on the jury found for the defense, declared the shooting justifiable, and turned McCall loose. The newspaper voiced the surprise and beliefs of many when the editor wrote, "Should it ever be our misfortune to kill a man, we would simply ask that our trial may take place in some of the mining camps of these hills."

The swaggering, bombastic Jack "Broken Nose" McCall lit out for Wyoming Territory. His braggadocio about killing Wild Bill would soon land him back in Dakota Territory, wishing he'd kept his mouth shut.

CHAPTER THIRTY

Among Wild Bill's closest acquaintances in Deadwood, only Calamity Jane stayed on. Colorado Charley Utter folded his tent and went back to Colorado. As for me, I dismissed any notion I'd had of hanging up my shingle and opening an undertaking parlor to serve the citizens of Deadwood. I'd had my fill of boomtowns, this one in particular, despite the opportunity it offered for the adventurous and enterprising young man.

Abilene, Pioche, Cheyenne, Deadwood — somehow their attractions had paled when compared to more settled and civilized places like Kansas City and Salt Lake City, although I disliked the anonymity of a sprawling metropolis. But, boredom and dullness and obscurity had become more enticing than the hurry-up and hurly-burly and accompanying violence of frontier boomtowns. If there was a brass ring to be grabbed in the Black Hills, someone else would have to grasp it.

When the trunk and cases and bags holding my embalming apparatus and the rest of my worldly goods arrived in Deadwood, I did not bother to unpack. Rather, I threw in with a group of disenchanted miners bound for home, loaded my possessions into one of the three wagons in their pitiful train, and set out through the Black Hills for points east, hoping against hope the recent battles between the Sioux and the United States Army had the Indians so occupied we would not be harassed.

Just where I would land I knew not.

When our ragtag wagon train made the far reaches of Dakota Territory and rolled into Yankton, I found myself so disheartened and weary I thought to give the town a try. It seemed as good as any.

Like so many American cities, Yankton took its name from the Indians who were pushed out to make room for white settlers. The small city, just north of three thousand residents, was, nevertheless, the capital city of the sprawling Dakota Territory that encompassed a big slice of what the nation acquired when Thomas Jefferson bought Louisiana from the French. The Plains Indians paid little attention to such claims of ownership, but the federal government in Washington was rapidly disabusing them of such notions, in this case by displacing the Yankton Sioux band that once lived here and warehousing them on a reservation some fifty miles west.

Much of the busy Missouri River traffic in those days tied up at Yankton to take on supplies and fresh water, and load up with upriver freight delivered to the capital city on the Dakota Southern Railway's tracks. The city was small, but prosperous.

And so I settled in Yankton, taking room and board with a Civil War widow named Lydia Krause and her daughter Miriam. Theirs was not a rooming house as such, me being the only regular tenant. Renting the room to me, with a second spare room kept available for a trio of traveling salesmen who came through Yankton, in turn, on a fairly predictable schedule, provided a livelihood for the two women.

It was a comfortable situation for me, particularly in light of the fact that I took up with Miriam. I found her company congenial, and she seemed to enjoy mine, once she got past the curiosity concerning my missing limb and the usual hesitation resulting from my line of work.

A small rented building on the bluffs

above the river, and not far from the Krause home, served for my business interests. Up front I set up a small office to meet the public, with two larger rooms in the back — one dedicated to undertaking and embalming, the other for woodworking. I manufactured coffins for my own use and offered others for sale and delivery elsewhere, as well as taking on small commercial cabinetry projects from time to time. A display advertisement in the *Yankton Daily Press & Dakotan* drew attention to the enterprise and enough customers to make the business pay, even if the living it provided was a modest one.

An item in that same newspaper caught my eye shortly after my arrival. According to the newspaper, Dakota territorial officials were horrified by the results of Jack McCall's trial in Deadwood. The trial and verdict were declared void, what with Deadwood lacking official sanction or jurisdiction. The US marshal assigned to the Territory ordered McCall tracked down, arrested, and brought to the capital to be tried for murder.

It did not take long. The murderer had not been able to resist adding to the ever-present wind in Wyoming Territory with a lot of hot air of his own. The newspaper wrote that a deputy US marshal quenching his thirst in a saloon in Laramie heard McCall bloviating on his prowess with a gun, as demonstrated by his killing of the legendary pistoleer Wild Bill Hickok. He only restrained his tongue when handcuffs bound his arms. McCall came to Yankton in chains and a federal judge put him on trial for murder, assigning a pair of lawyers to defend him.

I kept at my work, awaiting the trial. I intended to be in the gallery for every session. When the courthouse doors swung open on the first day of the trial, I was near the head of the line and found a seat near the front. An older man slid onto the bench beside me, jostling me as he scooted close to make room for others.

"Pardon me," he said.

It took me a moment to accept the apology as the man's appearance took my breath away. "Ex— excuse me, sir, but you — you look an awful lot like Wild Bill."

"That right?"

"Yes. Yes, it is."

"How do you know? You been looking at pictures of him?"

"No, sir. I knew Bill."

The man chuckled, but there wasn't much in the way of humor in the laugh. "You and everybody else."

Taken aback by his response, it again took me a moment to collect myself. "It's true. I did know him. Got to know him in Abilene when he was town marshal. Saw him again in Kansas City — he bought me a glass of lemonade at the Exposition. And I was in Deadwood with him when he was killed."

He asked about Wild Bill's death, and I told him what I had witnessed. He sat silent for a time, head bowed and fingers interlaced in his lap. I did not know if he was thinking or praying. It could well have been both.

"You telling me the truth?"

"Yes, sir."

"All of what you said?"

"Every word."

He extended his hand. I grasped it, he gripped my hand firmly, and we shook.

"The reason why I look like James — I don't call him 'Bill' — is that I am his brother. Lorenzo Butler Hickok."

"I am pleased to meet you, Mister Hickok."

The judge banged his gavel, calling the court to order. Like many in the audience, I suspect, I expected a lengthy and lively trial with much bombast. It turned out to be a businesslike affair and was over within two days.

McCall's lawyers had little to offer up in the way of a defense. The justification that got him off in Deadwood — that Wild Bill killed his brother — fell apart when the prosecution produced a woman who came from the same hometown as McCall. She swore under oath she had known him since they were children growing up, and that the accused had no brother. The jury found the defendant guilty of the murder of James Butler "Wild Bill" Hickok and the judge sentenced McCall to hang.

Lorenzo and I had become better acquainted over the two days of the trial, going so far as sharing supper. The day after the trial, I accompanied him to the train that would take him home to Illinois. "I won't be coming back for the hanging, son. I'm counting on you to see it's done right."

"I will do my best, mister Hickok."

He nodded and stepped onto the train.

All this happened at the onset of winter, but for reasons I was not privy to, the hanging did not occur until the verge of spring. In the interim, McCall rotted in jail. I went about my business, keeping as busy as I wanted to.

Winter in Yankton offered few distractions.

I spent many a long evening in Missus Krause's parlor, visiting with her and Miriam. Miriam was a reader, and our tastes in literature overlapped enough that there was always something to talk about. But, just as many evenings found me with my gouges and knives, turning a length of rare — and expensive — ebony into a new peg leg.

Working the ebony required more patience than I would have credited myself with. The black wood, so dense and heavy and hard, meant I spent as much time keeping tools sharp as I did carving. But winters are long and dark in Yankton, and the wood occupied my mind and my hands for many an hour that would not have been as profitably spent elsewhere.

Dakota Territory had never executed a man before, requiring the construction of a gallows. Winter on the courthouse square in Yankton was ushered out with the sound of handsaws and hammers. I took mean comfort in the fact that the only view through the barred window of Jack McCall's cell was of the rising scaffold that would prove his downfall.

When the appointed time for McCall's execution drew near, I paid a visit to the territorial marshal, whose job it was to oversee the hanging.

The marshal studied the card I handed him. "Jonathon 'Pinebox' Collins," he read. "Undertaker and Embalmer." His eyes met mine. "How can I help you, Mister Jonathon Pinebox Collins?"

"I'd like to volunteer my services."

His forehead furrowed, one eyebrow rising and the other falling, his pursed lips likewise angled. "How's that?"

"After you hang Jack McCall, I want to ready his remains for burial. At no expense to the Territory."

"Oh? Why's that?"

"I knew Wild Bill Hickok. Saw McCall gun him down, as it happens. I want to make damn sure the murdering coward is dead. Sounds strange, I know. Somehow, it feels like something I ought to do."

The marshal grinned a perplexed grin and shook his head. "Can't beat the price, that's for sure. I'll look into it and make sure there's no reason not to let you have your way."

I thanked the marshal, but worried when I did not hear from him.

Come the morning of the hanging, I came early to the courthouse to assure myself a view of the hanging, unobstructed by what was sure to be a sizeable crowd. Not knowing if it would be necessary, I drove there in my wagon and tied the horse to a hitching post across the square from the courthouse.

As I crossed the square, the marshal came out the door on the side of the courthouse that led to the jail. "Collins!" he yelled, hailing me with a wave of his hand.

He waited for me, and I angled over to where he stood. He pointed at my wagon. "That your meat wagon over there?"

I nodded.

"That horse of yours — he gentle?"

I nodded again.

"Not likely to be upset by the crowd milling about?"

I shook my head.

"Why don't you fetch it over here and park it under that tree there by the gallows? You'll have a good view of the hanging from the seat and it'll be handy to load McCall's body after."

I took that as meaning I would lay out the murderer as I had hoped, and hustled across the square and parked the wagon where the marshal said, attaching a tether weight to the bridle to discourage the horse from any temptation to wander. Not that it was likely — the old horse would most likely sleep through the whole affair.

As the crowd assembled, I allowed several people — some I had seen on the streets of

Yankton over the months, and some I did not recognize — to sit or stand in the back of the wagon. And while it did not give me any great comfort to do so, I invited Missus Krause and Miriam to join me on the seat.

As the courthouse clock tolled ten, the marshal and two of his deputies, each carrying a shotgun, escorted the prisoner out of the jail door. A priest clutching a Bible brought up the rear. McCall's hands were bound behind him. Face pale and eyes wide, he studied the faces in the crowd as the onlookers parted to allow the lawman and murderer to pass. Even given the size of the crowd, it grew so silent on the square you could hear the limbs on the tree — there were no leaves as yet — rattle in the breeze.

The marshal pushed McCall into the lead and his escort followed him up the thirteen steps. The deputies moved to opposite corners of the front of the scaffold, taking up a port arms position with their scatter guns. The marshal stopped McCall near the trap door, where he dropped to his knees. The priest knelt beside him and they talked to one another in whispers. The marshal knelt as well, but with a different purpose — he pulled a short length of rope from his belt and tied the condemned prisoner's ankles together.

Grabbing McCall by an elbow, he lifted him to his feet and pushed him onto the trap. He slipped a black hood over the prisoner's head, followed by the noose, which he snugged up tight. He let the slack droop below McCall's shoulder.

Then came McCall's voice, muffled but easy enough to hear. "Draw it tighter, Marshal."

With another tug to tighten the noose, the marshal stepped to the lever, took a deep breath, and sprung the trap. McCall dropped through the hole, bounced once when the rope snapped taut, and turned slowly to the right.

The clock on the tower read 10:10, the hands forming a V, pointing the way, I thought, to the hell where Jack McCall's soul now resided.

As the still-quiet crowd dispersed, a doctor made his way to the hanging body, climbed upon a box, and checked McCall for signs of life, of which there were none. The marshal stood on the gallows, watching down the hole. He sent his deputies down to hold the dangling body, pulled a jack-knife from his pocket, and sliced through the hanging rope.

The deputies let the body turn horizontal and carried it, one holding the legs, the other with his arms wrapped around Mc-Call's chest, in which no heart beat nor breath moved. They swung him onto the back of the wagon, and shifted him around until he was lengthwise, leaving his head bagged and tossing the tail of the rope onto the wagon bed. I fetched a folded tarpaulin from under the seat, stepped over and unfurled the cloth, and draped it over the body. Miriam and Missus Krause stood by watching as this unfolded. I unsnapped the tether weight, dropped it under the wagon seat, and climbed aboard. With a tip of the hat to the ladies, I snapped the lines over the horse's rump and he plodded his way up the bluff to my undertaking parlor.

Jack McCall, evil though he was, received the same respectful care in washing, embalming, and dressing that all remains trusted to my care did.

With one exception.

If, at some future date, the body of Jack McCall should be disinterred, and the coffin prized open, those inspecting his remains will find the hangman's noose still around his neck.

CHAPTER THIRTY-ONE

The next year or two in Yankton found me settling into day-to-day life in the city as a regular citizen. Mine was a familiar, if unremarkable, face on the streets, my peg leg part of the recognition. The undertaking business proved profitable, and "those coffins of Pinebox's," most made from any wood but pine, found their way onto steamboats and rail cars for shipment to undertakers in other towns and cities.

I stayed on at Missus Krause's, even though my income and savings would allow the purchase or construction of a home of my own. I enjoyed living there, particularly the presence of Miriam. That we were discussing matrimony more and more frequently added to the pleasure of the accommodations.

And then one day a six-word telegram arrived, return address: Calamity Jane, Deadwood.

Come. Got to move Wild Bill.

"How on earth did you find me, Jane?"

"Aw, hell, Pinebox. I can read. We get a Yankton newspaper up here every now and then, and I see your advertisements in there. Didn't take no Pinkerton man to find you."

A similar telegram reached Charley Utter.

"What is it, Calamity? What do you mean we've got to move Bill?"

"That Ingleside Cemetery is filled to overflowin' and Wild Bill's bein' crowded out. 'Sides that, folks is all the time disturbin' his grave. They've whittled and chipped away at his marker till there ain't hardly a damn thing left of it. Hell, some of them people even take away a scoop of dirt from the grave. Beats me why they do it, but it ain't proper."

Utter nursed a whiskey and contemplated Jane's words as we sat at a table in Nuttal & Mann's Saloon. Jane had downed several shots. I sipped slowly at a beer, uncomfortable with my presence in the place.

"What do you suggest we do?" Utter said.

"There's a new boneyard," Jane said. "Mount Moriah, they call it."

Naming a cemetery in Deadwood for the mountain in the Holy Land where Abraham meant to sacrifice Isaac brought a wry smile

343

to my face, but I held my peace.

"We need to buy a plot there, Charley. A big one. Put a fence around it. Put up a new marker. Plant ol' Bill under it, and leave room to plant yours truly when I cash in my chips." Jane threw back another shot of whiskey. "It was Wild Bill's wish that we lay side by side in eternal rest, y'know."

We visited Bill's grave at Ingleside, and Jane had a point about the desecration of his resting place. But what she really wanted was for Colorado Charley to foot the bill for her plan. And he did, less a small contribution from my bank account.

Come time to effect the move, we hired a team of gravediggers and a dray to help. I was not surprised to see Wild Bill's coffin in a sorry state. Pierce's shoddy construction allowed it to leak like a sieve and the wood was sorely decayed. It crumbled further when the workers threaded ropes underneath and attempted to raise it. I say "attempt" deliberately, as the men, despite much strain and struggle, were unable to lift what was left of Bill and his box.

It took more ropes and more men — recruited from among the crowd of curiosity seekers — to shift it. The sexton and workers argued over the weight — some claiming four hundred pounds, others estimating it as high as five hundred. The why of it spawned even more debate, which turned to wonder when we lifted the lid — which came off in pieces — to reveal the corpse.

Wild Bill looked to be well preserved, but something looked amiss. One of the onlookers tapped Bill's folded hands with a walking stick and it sounded for all the world like he was rapping a marble marker. I knelt by the body and felt of it, caressing the skin of his hands and face, and palpating the chest and thighs.

Wild Bill Hickok was, in fact, as hard as a rock.

The only explanation, although it did not seem reasonable to me, was that Wild Bill was petrified. If such a thing was possible, I attributed it to the sorry job of embalming, which may have allowed chemical compounds in the soil and water to invade the body, the result being the petrification — or whatever it was — of Bill's remains.

There's one thing to remember about me: a man in my line of work grows accustomed to drinking alone — even here in Yankton, where I am well known. As a practitioner of The Dismal Trade, I may not be shunned in the city but my company in social situations is seldom sought.

And so I have gained the habit over the years of spending my evenings at otherwise empty tables in the far corners of saloons where I can view the festivities from the partial concealment of dim lamplight. This evening, my grog shop of choice is the Riverside Saloon on Third Street.

It has been a long day.

Two "customers" arrived at my undertaking parlor today, one a sometime wharf worker and full-time alcoholist who drowned when an excess of drink caused — or contributed to — his falling into the Missouri River. His was not the first such body I have laid to rest in Yankton owing to the same cause. Even more tragic, I was entrusted with the mortal remains of a child of six years old, lost to a fever.

As I sip a beer turning tepid and losing its foam, I drag a chair away from the table and place it where I can comfortably prop my peg leg on it an attempt to relieve the ache in my thigh and hip. Even now, these years later, I cannot help but admire the wooden leg.

I believe it is my finest, and so satisfied am I with it that I have yet to even contemplate fashioning another.

Its polished ebony gleams in the hazy

light, and as I rock it back and forth on the chair seat, highlights glint across its surfaces. Carved in deep relief on the front side is a playing card — the ace of spades. On the outside surface is sculpted the ace of clubs. The inside and back of the prosthesis show the eight of clubs and the eight of spades. Those particular poker cards have become most famous in the long and violent history of our fading frontier.

They call it the "dead man's hand."

And I, as well as anyone and better than most, know why.

AUTHOR'S NOTE

Pinebox Collins is a work of fiction. While readers with more than a passing familiarity with the history of the Old West will recognize that many of the characters and events in its pages are historically based, it is fiction, not history. I have taken many liberties, particularly with chronology, and several of the characters are my creations. That aside, I have made every attempt to make the people and places true to the times.

ABOUT THE AUTHOR

Winner of four Western Writers of America Spur Awards and a Spur Award finalist on six other occasions, **Rod Miller** writes fiction, poetry, and history about the American West. A lifelong Westerner raised in a cowboy family, Miller is a former rodeo contestant, worked in radio and television production, and is a retired advertising agency copywriter and creative director. *Pinebox Collins* is his seventh novel and fifteenth book. Miller's award-winning poetry and short stories have appeared in numerous anthologies, and several magazines have carried his byline.